OBSTACLE COURSE

YVONNE MONTGOMERY

AVON BOOKS ◆ NEW YORK

For Betsy Cox and Pat Doi:
a memorial to the paths
through the forest.

OBSTACLE COURSE is an original publication of Avon Books. This work has never before appeared in book form. This work is a novel. Any similarity to actual persons or events is purely coincidental.

AVON BOOKS
A division of
The Hearst Corporation
105 Madison Avenue
New York, New York 10016

Copyright © 1990 by Yvonne Montgomery
Published by arrangement with the author
Library of Congress Catalog Card Number: 90-93178
ISBN: 0-380-75992-6

All rights reserved, which includes the right to reproduce this book or portions thereof in any form whatsoever except as provided by the U.S. Copyright Law. For information address Meredith Bernstein Literary Agency, 2112 Broadway, Suite 503A, New York, New York 10023.

First Avon Books Printing: December 1990

AVON TRADEMARK REG. U.S. PAT. OFF. AND IN OTHER COUNTRIES, MARCA REGISTRADA, HECHO EN U.S.A.

Printed in the U.S.A.

RA 10 9 8 7 6 5 4 3 2 1

OBSTACLE COURSE

Landauer started toward her. By the look on his face, Finny didn't have any doubts about whether he was capable of violence.

"I think it would be to your advantage to conduct your inquiries elsewhere," Landauer said menacingly. "It has nothing to do with me."

Finny didn't particularly relish being close enough to him to count the pores in his chiseled nose. She took a step back.

"I wish you well in your efforts to help your friend," Landauer went on. "I can't imagine why she would lie about a murder. But I hope that she did . . . for your sake!" The door shut sharply behind him.

My, my, thought Finny. It looked like it was time to pick up speed in the old recreational snooping—time to find out what the hell was going on.

"WIT AND INSIGHT . . .
SHOULD APPEAL TO FANS OF MARTHA GRIMES"
Mystery News

Other Avon Books by
Yvonne Montgomery

SCAVENGERS

Avon Books are available at special quantity discounts for bulk purchases for sales promotions, premiums, fund raising or educational use. Special books, or book excerpts, can also be created to fit specific needs.

For details write or telephone the office of the Director of Special Markets, Avon Books, Dept. FP, 105 Madison Avenue, New York, New York 10016, 212-481-5653.

One

THE FOOD on the table was enough to feed a small, starving nation, not that the faceless in extremis would have been able to digest it. *Escargots embrouillés* and truffles, garlic, and Gruyère required systems hardened through long practice: only the jaded need apply.

Finny Aletter let her fingers do the grazing through the morsels tenderly nested in artifice. The mallard hewn in ice was laden with melon balls big enough to serve over a net. Radish roses and botanically impossible blossoms carved from celery stalks and carrot sticks bloomed among bacon-wrapped water chestnuts and cheese that had been teased into shapes no cheese was ever meant to be. Nuggets of fruit and pink morsels of shrimp had been stabbed artistically onto stainless-steel skewers with rosewood handles.

"Who does your nails?"

Finny glanced from her carpentry-branded hands to the source of the light, insolent voice. A young woman, frizzily blonde, met her eyes with a don't-give-a-damn expression. Malice was at least as responsible as Estée Lauder for whatever life her features held.

"Black & Decker," Finny said.

"Is that the new place in Cherry Creek? Hope you didn't leave a tip." Boredom won out over malice and the blonde slinked her way back into the social sediment, her strapless black cocktail gown a moving challenge to several laws of God and physics.

One of those laws, thought Finny, was that there was

1

always somebody who could zero in on your insecurities like a shark could scent blood. She'd always valued competence over beauty—a safe bet since she boasted only moderate stature; short, black hair instead of the long, pampered blonde stuff; and features that elicited tributes such as "animated" and "attractive." She'd known she was underdressed as soon as she walked in the door. The promised casual gathering had been translated into an understated fashion parade. The swimming pool shimmering through the gauzy drapes over the patio doors seemed as distant as the tropical sea it had been designed to evoke, as unapproachable as the sleek, satisfied "natives."

"Who the hell was that?" Chris Barelli was tall, dark, and conservative in his pale gray suit, snowy white shirt, and striped tie. His venture to the bar had left him unmarked, his thick black hair falling over his forehead, his strong features impenetrable, his large hands steady with their burden of brimming wineglasses. The eyes that noticed everything had darkened with scientific interest at the amount of torque in the blonde's hips.

"There wasn't time to exchange names before she opened fire." It had been a while since she'd been offered entrée into Denver's hallowed halls of society. The invitations she'd come to expect as an up-and-coming stockbroker dried up after her involvement in a murder investigation the year before. The same people who would kill for a mention in the society columns underwent immediate profile surgery when another's name cropped up on the police blotter.

Finny sipped her drink and surveyed the living room of the house that had been called "Tara on a half lot." It had roughly the proportions of a basketball court but smelled much better. Tall, cafe au lait walls wore their paintings and etchings like a bourgeoise choosing jewelry for a meeting with the queen: too much was never enough.

Wide walkways of bank lobby marble edged steps descending, Roman-style, on all four sides to the central area of the room. Thick, butter yellow carpet stretched like redemption across the aptly named conversation pit, under soft sculpture furniture and hard-edged people. The individual chatter was carefully modulated but the aggregate effect had Excedrin written all over it. Any lull in the roar was filled by the anemic musical offerings of a wilted string quartet bunched in a corner at the far end of the room.

Finny recognized a number of the people in the crowd. The two three-piece suits who had staked out the organically shaped love seat near the string quartet had been clients: one a banker, the other of the nouveau entrepreneurial class. Nearby, three people—a nervous man sandwiched between two women, all brokers in competing firms—were wielding their smiles as shields, their ears alert to the nuances of the insider tidbits sprinkled throughout the conversation like spices in ragout. Their rapid consumption of alcohol attested to the strain of the concentration needed to determine the validity of what was said and, more important, what was not said. The schizophrenia of the Dow Jones had etched their faces like acid.

And to think, she hadn't wanted to be here this evening. She reached past Barelli for a fat scallop speared on a tutu-clad toothpick.

"Finny, darling!" Twee Garrett spoke in small, honey-eyed tones that lowered people's eyes in expectation of a short, rounded woman. Her Valkyrie height and linebacker presence came as a distinct surprise, especially when clad, as tonight, in the ruffles the voice implied.

"You're late, you naughty girl. Everyone's been here for at least an hour."

"Sorry," Finny said around the scallop in her mouth. "I had to wait for—"

"Never explain." Twee's vivid green gaze roamed over her. "You look smashing, as always. If there were any chance that I could fit into that gorgeous raspberry silk, I'd rip it right off your back. Why wasn't I born a brunette?"

"This old thing?" Finny laughed lightly, glancing down at the polyester blend shirt belted casually over the matching circle skirt, both of which she'd snatched yesterday afternoon off a sale rack at Stein Mart.

Twee shook her bouffant, lavender-gray coif briskly. "You're supposed to be working the room, dearest, convincing these moneyed darlings that they cannot *live* without your services." She flashed a strobe-brilliant smile at Barelli, who took a step back in self-defense. "Who is this enchanting man?"

"Twee, I'd like you to meet my friend Chris Barelli," Finny said. "This is our hostess, Chris, Twee Garrett."

Twee grasped Barelli's hand with long tapered fingers. "So nice to meet you at last," she burbled with genuine warmth. "You're Finny's *very* good friend, aren't you? The policeman?"

At Barelli's nod, the fretwork of lines that webbed the corners of Twee's smile deepened. "You've been *so* good for this child. She was just drying up with those dreadful people at L and F. She was always much too creative to be satisfied with being a stockbroker, don't you agree?"

The wariness on Barelli's face mellowed into a smile as he read her eyes, on a level with his own. "Absolutely," he began, then stopped at the crash from across the room that cut through the haze of party gabble like a sword through satin.

"Oh, dear." Twee pressed Barelli's shoulder with a diamond-laden hand. "The new girl simply has no idea of how to balance a tray. Do excuse me, darlings, I'll be *right* back."

"Good lord," Barelli said as Twee surged away through the crush around the table.

"Yes." Finny drained her glass. "You see now why I had to come?"

"It was either that or hop a plane for Rio. Where in God's name did you meet her?"

"She was one of my clients, one of the first I ever had."

"And you left her to the barracudas at L and F?"

"She moved her account to Charton and Wells right after I left." Finny set her glass beside the others decorating the base of an anatomically correct but eccentrically arranged sculpture of a man, a woman, and a cape. "But she just about killed me when I quit L and F—said she'd never speak to me again."

Barelli glanced around Twee's version of the Roman circus. "But—"

"She's a very sweet woman. Now she's convinced it was all her idea."

"So she throws you a party—"

"—to get all of her friends to hire me," Finny finished for him. "Greasing the wheels of my success."

"More like the skids." Barelli's mouth tightened at another whinny of laughter from the mass below them. He didn't bother lowering his voice. "Do you think you're going to get anywhere with a bunch of chinless wonders like—"

"Excuse me."

The man who loomed next to her was more beautiful than most of the women in the room, Finny realized as her gaze was caught by deep blue eyes. Tan of skin, Slavic of cheekbones, sculpted of nose, he was perfection clad in an unstructured maize jacket over a flowing aqua shirt tucked into pleated oatmeal linen slacks that fit well enough to make any woman worth her salt dream of taking them off. If Tom Selleck ever saw this guy, his dimples would drop out, Finny mused, but she retained the presence of mind to look pointedly at his square, cleft chin and raise a brow at Barelli.

"You are Finny Aletter aren't you?" His smile rewarded her for being both female and attractive, hinting at unknown rewards lying in wait for an affirmative answer.

Finny nodded.

"I'm Kit Landauer. Twee asked me to come over here and tell you 'Faint heart never won renovation jobs.'" His broad shoulders moved in a desultory shrug and Finny struggled with an excess of esthetic appreciation. "Do you have any idea what she meant?"

"You're simpering," murmured Barelli in her ear.

Finny glared at him and pulled herself together. "I renovate old houses and Twee decided she wanted to, uh—"

"Sponsor you?" The interest in Landauer's eyes deepened. He tilted his head, his golden curls gleaming in the soft light of the candles on the table. "Interior design, huh? I'm in the business myself. What kind of things have you done?"

"I'm a carpenter," Finny said, pulling her gaze away from him at the nudge at her arm. "Uh, this is my friend Chris Barelli."

"Barelli." Landauer extended a sun-bronzed hand. The thick, burnished links of his gold ID bracelet shifted with the motion. "Haven't I seen you at the club?"

"Which club is that?"

"The Summit Club." The shades of disbelief in his rugged baritone suggested a crisis in understanding; there were other clubs?

"Not unless you've had a murder there recently." At his expression of blank confusion, Barelli took pity on him. "I'm a cop. Denver Homicide."

"Oh." Landauer's expression slid into neutral. "Then, of course, you wouldn't have been there."

Landauer turned to Finny, his perfect smile diminished. "So nice to have met you. Perhaps we'll see each other again sometime." He didn't wait for Finny to return his civilities, moving on with manly determination toward the bar.

Barelli watched his departure, shifting aside for a man intent upon the shrimp. He slanted a glance at Finny. "Didn't mean to slow you down, babe."

"I wasn't aware that you had."

He looked down his straight nose at her, one brow lifted. "Wipe the saliva off your chin." He grinned as her hand moved reflexively, then returned to her side.

Finny bared her teeth in a smile. "I'm not dead, Chris. I noticed you didn't resist ogling the blonde with the—"

"Breasts." The nearby angular woman in puce flashed him a glance and moved quickly past the melon balls.

"Among other things."

He nodded. "But I'm not hawking my wares, babe. A cool dude plus a sharp cookie—you could be home free with someone like Landauer backing your play."

"What play is that?"

"You could have any one of these bozos eating out of your hand. Bat the old eyelashes a little bit—"

"Wiggle my tush?" Finny raised a brow. "I'm into carpentry—the nobility of manual labor—not turning tricks. You been spending your off hours on the vice detail?"

"You're missing the point, babe. You want to make it with the big guys, you cut loose the excess baggage."

"You ain't heavy, you're my—well, you get my drift." Finny's gaze narrowed. "And what the hell is this 'sharp cookie' crap? You know I wasn't too thrilled about coming here tonight. So why get bent out of shape by some *GQ*-type?"

"Call it common sense on top of experience." Barelli's tone was dry. "If you're going to be class conscious, cops ain't got no—"

"Finny." Twee thundered back into the magic circle. "I simply won't *allow* you to stay here by the hors d'oeuvres while all these potential clients are milling around." Her hand closed on Finny's arm. "Come with me, darling." She pulled her away a few steps, then checked over her shoulder. "Aren't you coming with us, Lieutenant?"

Barelli's smile was infinitesimal. "I'm having such a good conversation with the hors d'oeuvres."

Twee threw him a roguish look, then dragged Finny into an animated forest of silk and linen, jersey and chiffon.

Finny had never felt so on display. Twee was as voluble as a carnival hawker as she towed her from group to group, pointing out her assets with relish, underscoring her move from stockbroker to carpenter, stressing her unique qualifications for translating the construction wishes of these "moneyed darlings," too long beset with learning-disabled lowlifes. As Finny followed Twee's black-and-silver ruffles from cluster to cluster of polite smiles and bored eyes, she wondered if perhaps her place in the carnival was the sideshow.

"Les Trethalwyn of the Denver Arts Consortium." Twee was identifying the stocky, bearded man who stood close to an enigmatic, willowy vision in burgundy silk.

He bent over Finny's extended hand and mimed a kiss above her knuckles. Several sandy curls fell over his damp brow. "A pleasure." There was a smooth purr of interest in his voice.

Hmmm. Finny turned as the introductions continued. "And this is my godchild, Paige Dexter." Twee's face shone with fierce pride. "She's got the most divine English garden and it's positively crying out for a gazebo."

Paige Dexter had broken off her conversation with Trethalwyn to listen to Twee. She now turned her smooth, brown head to look at Finny, her almond-shaped eyes opaque. As if counting with an internal rhythm, she waited until the small silence among them swelled to the point of discomfort, then allowed her thin lips to curve into what could pass for a smile.

"Another protégée, Twee?" she drawled. "Whatever happened to the landscape artist—Jose, wasn't it?" Her impenetrable eyes, in contrast to her slow speech, darted over Finny in rapid, precise assessment.

What a bundle this broad could make on "The Price is Right," Finny mused. Too bad she was wasted on the social circuit.

Not that she languished in obscurity. Everyone had heard of Paige Dexter, long-time patron saint of the Dare to Care Festival. Spending three dollars for every dollar raised, her group of ministering angels had recently adopted two uncharacteristically useful charities: fighting illiteracy and fostering animals abandoned in the Denver metropolitan area. Society watchers of a more cynical bent yearned for a merging of the two efforts.

"I don't really know that I'm ready to consider the gazebo, Twee." Paige's smile acknowledged the deepening color in Twee's face, then gathered itself into a moué of mocking realization as her expressionless eyes encountered Finny's flat gaze. "Unless it's a question of survival. If you truly *need* the money. . . ."

"Please," Finny said pleasantly. "No noblesse oblige: it's terrible for the digestion." She'd been afraid of something like this when Twee had broached the idea of her "coming out" party. As a stockbroker she'd worked with a few scions of Denver society—enough to be aware of the awkwardness when business and blue blood mixed. And her blood was of a decidedly reddish cast. A few of the Old Money types still existed, but increasing numbers of the younger society people were nouveau riche, and the collar color switch might hit a bit too close to home.

Before Paige could verbalize the petulance expressed on her face, Les Trethalwyn entered the fray. "So, you expect me to believe that such a feminine creature as yourself is a carpenter?" The softened burr of his Welsh accent held amusement. "I must say that you American women are astonishingly versatile."

"Finny more than most," Twee assured him. "She was the best broker I ever had. She could read my *mind*."

"Surely that stood you in good stead during the murder investigation." Paige angled her chin toward Les. "In addition to her other activities, Miss Aletter solved a murder." She raised a brow. "I'm surprised that you didn't go into police work as opposed to construction."

I'd love to see *you* in a holding cell, Finny thought. "I don't have the stomach for it," she said. "Too much grief."

"One would think that the challenge would be almost irresistible." Paige parted with another ersatz smile. "You must have enjoyed the . . . acclaim you received in the papers."

"No," Finny said. "I prefer to keep my good deeds to myself. As I'm sure you do."

Paige's sculpted cheeks darkened. She had been featured prominently in both Denver dailies that week, and not by accident.

"Well," Twee said uncomfortably, "perhaps we'd better spread you around a little more, Finny."

"Sic transit mayonnaise." Finny nodded to Les Trethalwyn. "Happy to meet you." Her polite smile shifted into sincerity at the twinkle in his brown eyes. Then another nod. "Ms. Dexter."

Finny lay a hand on Twee's arm as they neared the next group. "I need a quick break: I think I'll visit the restroom. Shall I meet you back here?"

"Oh, uh, yes." Twee's usual ebullience was dimmed. "I'm sorry," she said. "About Paige, I mean. She can be rather abrupt at times. I'm sure she didn't mean—"

"Don't worry about it. Maybe she's having an off night.

I'll be back in a bit." Finny wove her way deftly through the snarls of people, toward the beckoning refuge of the powder room. Twee could kid herself all she liked. Paige Dexter was a third-rate imitation of Morgan le Fay, and the only hired help she would ever need was a full-time PR agent to help her avoid cutting her own throat with her serrated tongue.

She'd nearly made good her escape when a hand clamped onto her arm, stopping her in her tracks.

"Well, as I live and breathe." The smooth voice was as unexpected as a burst of swamp gas, and every bit as salutary. "Finny Aletter, the Wonder Woman of Seventeenth Street."

Two

FINNY LOOKED into the face from the past without revealing how unwelcome it was. "Hello, Ty."

Ty Engelman was a reminder of a particularly dead-end time in her life, when her work at Lakin & Fulton had been the only thing between her and the kind of slow-slide depression that gets expressed in too much booze and bad-judgment sex. She'd met him at a retirement party and had been impressed by both his ambition and his flair. Denver was just a way station for him, and Wall Street wouldn't know what hit it when he got there.

But things never went Ty's way. He was the kind of man drawn to self destruction like a leech to warm flesh. He'd told her his plans during that year he worked down the street, as constant as a vulture, always on the lookout for a lunch date, always ready with the lure of concert tickets or that perfect late night hideaway. And he was always on the verge of the one magical deal promising to reinvent his world, unlocking the door to Arbitrage Heaven.

He had drifted away soon after Finny bought her house. It had taken her a long time to figure out that she'd lost her usefulness as a co-conspirator in Ty's self-sabotage.

It surprised her to see how healthy he looked: his blue-black hair, combed away from the narrow forehead in a wave, was untouched by silver. A streamlined bone structure was the underlay for pale, still-supple skin; the poetically large, dark eyes glowed with an inner flame. It was almost as if no time had passed between their meetings. A pact with the devil, perhaps, speculated Finny.

More likely a close relationship with a talented plastic surgeon.

"I heard you quit L and F," Ty was saying. "Did you take Twee with you when you left?"

"Nobody 'takes' Twee anyplace." Finny glanced around for one of the drink trays that waiters had been carrying through the crowd periodically. "She's decided to make me the new fashion in carpenters."

"Carpenters?" Ty's lips curled in amused disbelief. "What's the scam?"

"No scam. I renovate houses now."

"Oh, sweetheart, pull the other one." He laughed, loudly enough to draw the eyes of those around them. "You had ambition leaking out of your ears. What happened—you get sacked when the recession hit?"

"Like you?" Finny watched with satisfaction as the jeering amusement in his eyes flashed into anger. "No, I just got bored with the rat race. Such a cheesy life." Why did such conversations always spring upon you when you didn't have a drink? "Uh, what are you doing now?"

The wrinkle across Ty's forehead smoothed. "A little of this, and little of that. The economy's been a real bitch, hasn't it? The prospects are good—we just have to wait it out."

"You were always something of a BS artist," Finny said. "It can't have been too bad for you."

"Not so bad that I had to go into construction."

She might have deserved it, but she didn't have to stick around for more. "Well, it's been real." Finny extended her hand for the farewell grasp, only to have it pushed out of the way as Paige Dexter glided between her and Engelman, her own hand outstretched.

"Ty, how good to see you again."

Finny was amazed at the transformation of the woman. Her words were as formal as the proffered hand, but the Nefertiti profile had melted, replaced by a woman whose warmth escaped from the stiff image as rays of light beam from an eclipsed sun. Paige flicked an ill-feigned glance of surprise over one shoulder. "Oh, are you still hawking your wares, Miss—*what* was your name?"

"Never mind." Finny smiled pleasantly. "Mustn't overload the circuits." She looked at Engelman, and her smile died. His eyes were trained on Paige Dexter with painful intensity. "See you around, Ty," she said. He didn't hear her.

Finny do-si-doed her way through the gaggle: "Excuse me, I beg your pardon, oops, sorry," bouncing like a pinball from one conversation group to another.

"—served in the corner and the linesman called it—"

"—ermine, my you-know-what. She couldn't tell ermine from—"

"—too Club Med, my dear, and the service was shocking—"

Mouths were in motion under eyes that surveyed the room like lighthouse beams. Finny caught the incurious gazes that glanced off her and moved on to the next variation on the scene. What qualifications were required to rate a look of recognition, let alone to light up a face with welcome? Whatever they were, she didn't have them.

Tonight would drive a stake through any errant kindly memory she might have of life in the express lane. She changed direction at the nearby sound of Twee's dulcet tones, jostling the drinking arm of a silver-haired pinstriper. Burgundy splashed an instant Rorschach test over the snowy white of his shirt and did nothing to enhance the pattern of scalloped shells on his pale yellow tie.

"Oh, hell, I'm sorry." Finny glanced up at the man's face: it was rapidly turning the same hue as the spilled wine. She looked around quickly for a napkin. "Perhaps if there's some club soda," she began.

"Don't trouble yourself. I doubt if your club soda will work on silk." He glared fiercely at her. The smooth reddish gray eyebrows that matched thick, conservatively cut hair thundered over stormy brown eyes, his aquiline nose wrinkled against the malodor of clumsiness. "My dear young woman," issued from tight lips. "It's considered good manners to look where you're going."

"Dad, it was an accident," said the young woman beside him. She was elegant in her simplicity, smooth ginger hair curved around delicate features, a flowing ivory shirt tucked into a long purple gathered skirt emblazoned with a geometric pattern along the bottom edge. Then she smiled at Finny, and her face broke from elegance into cockeyed charm, mischief in the one twisted corner of her mouth, humor in the appleseed brown eyes. "I'm Cuffy Sarandon. This is my father, William Sarandon."

"Mr. Sarandon—"

"Judge." He pulled furiously at the handkerchief hiding from him in the inside pocket of his suit jacket.

"I really am sorry about the spill," Finny continued quietly. "Of course I'll take care of the cleaning expenses."

"That won't be necessary." One narrow hand dabbed ineffectually at the livid stain. "I see no reason to further our association." He pushed through the clutch of suits and designer togs next to them, then marched toward the doorway behind the refreshment table.

Cuffy Sarandon shot a look of embarrassed disbelief after her father. "I'm sorry. He usually prides himself on his manners."

"Then it's even harder to deal with clumsiness." Finny glanced down at the yellow rug: no stains, thank God. "At least I can replace his shirt."

"Don't count on it." Cuffy's smile folded at the corners. "I think he orders them from Europe—specially woven by Austrian silkworms or something."

"Hell." Finny met her gaze. "What can I do to make amends?"

"Believe me, one shirt's not going to make any difference. He's got enough shirts to last him till judgment day. Ah, the relief column's in sight."

Finny's gaze followed hers to the waiter skirting the edge of the crowd with a tray of stemware full of champagne. Cuffy signaled and they exchanged their empty glasses for two that were filled.

"These dos of Twee's get bigger all the time. I don't know where she finds the energy."

The champagne glow allowed Finny to smile. "I haven't been to any lately. I think the main reason Twee got excited about my new career was that it gave her an excuse to party."

Knowledge registered on Cuffy's face. "You're the lady carpenter. I'm sorry, I've forgotten your name."

"Finny Aletter. Considering your father's feelings, you probably ought to forget it again."

"You really don't have to feel so guilty, you know. He's not upset about the shirt." Cuffy sipped at the champagne. "He's taken a real beating this week, what with the papers and TV people hounding him."

The pieces fell into place. Judge William Sarandon had overseen a particularly nasty rape trial for the past two months. A young woman had been taken captive by a sex offender who was out on parole for the second time. He had abused her both sexually and psychologically for three days and had subsequently pleaded innocence by reason of temporary insanity. After weeks of acrimonious testimony from both prosecution and defense witnesses, the beleaguered jury had voted to convict the accused on all counts. The media had been filled with issues raised by the trial: insanity pleas, the parole system, even the political battle shaping up over increasing state spending on prison space.

At the guilty verdict, the relief and vindication of the victim and her family had turned to shocked outrage when Judge Sarandon announced the sentence. After pointing out that the victim had participated in her own attack by not attempting to escape from the apartment where she'd been held, the good judge had imposed the minimum mandatory sentence. The brouhaha that mushroomed in the wake of the judge's stab at Socratic wisdom was reminiscent of the lynch mob justice of Colorado's earlier history.

"The Elena Parmetter case," Finny said. What a pity she hadn't had a barrel of wine. She would have delighted in pushing the judge into it.

"Uh-huh." Cuffy's eyes met Finny's gaze with elaborate unconcern. "That's your cue to leave if you want to. Associating with a Sarandon isn't the best strategy for someone trying to give her business a boost."

"You aren't your father. Why should I blame you for what he did?"

"You'd be surprised at how many people think they can get to him through me." Cuffy's smile twisted. "A fat lot they know."

"People think they own you when there's some notoriety about you," Finny said. "Even if it's not your own. It's as though you owe them something for bringing yourself to their attention."

Recognition tinged the touch-me-not expression in Cuffy's eyes. "And you'd better not try to withhold payment."

"Sometimes it's better just to keep a low profile. When it comes right down to it, people have a hell of a short attention span."

"Is that what you did when Elliot Fulton was killed?"

"You remember that? Yeah, that's what I did." Finny glanced from her empty glass to Cuffy's. "You want some more champagne?"

"Sure. I can get it."

"Let me." Finny lifted Cuffy's glass out of her hand. "Stay put or I'll drink it all myself."

"It's a deal."

TRIP WIRE

SHE CLUTCHED the small white apron, now twisted at the waist of her black uniform. Her breath came in short, hard gasps.

His hand clamped onto her arm with the power of fear. *"Bianca! What the hell happened?"*

The girl brought one trembling hand up to her heart. "He started touching my . . . my breasts." Her swallow was loud in the quiet. "I do not like this, Miguel."

"Dammit, that was the whole point. He had to be doing something or the pictures wouldn't mean shit."

Her voice was a thread. *"Comprendo,* but—"

After a moment her breathing slowed, and she noticed he was rubbing his fingers. "You hurt your hand? When you hit him?"

"Yeah. It was worth it." They both looked down again at the man lying at their feet.

There was a whisper of sound, and Bianca cast a quick glance over her shoulder toward the back door. She could see the dull sheen of the aluminum screen door, but no one was standing there; no one was watching. Shivering, she was grateful for the thick shadows that seemed to crouch around the green glimmer of the pool. "You think he saw you?" she asked in a thready voice.

"I don't think so." His glance skittered around the yard. "We'd better move it."

She touched his arm. "What do we do now?"

"I'd like to kill the *cabron*."

"Miguel!"

"He deserves at least that for the damage he's done to Elena." He took a deep breath. "Come on, we can't do the pictures now. Let the sonofabitch sleep it off."

"You think he will make trouble when he wakes up?"

"He won't even remember your face." He urged her along the flagstone walk, then up the terraced deck to the back door of the house. He stopped to pick up the camera he'd left on the top step, then nudged her through the open door and toward the kitchen. "To them, you're part of the furniture. They don't know you're alive."

"Senora Garrett, she isn't like that . . ." Their voices blended into the party sounds that leaked from the doorway.

The soft lapping of the pool accompanied a cricket's musings. After a few minutes a shadow separated itself from the edge of the shade cast by the house and glided across the flat carpet of the lawn. The hazy light from the bottom of the pool reflected off the narrow shining surface of the skewer that swung like a pendulum at the shadow's side.

Three

WAITERS COULDN'T have been scarcer if they'd been named on the list of endangered species.

Finny tightened her hold on the glasses and slid around one chattering group and aimed for the bar. Cuffy seemed far too nice to have a Neanderthal like William Sarandon for a father. She grimaced. Sins of the father and all that rot.

She made like a sardine through the packed bodies, the noise a living thing now, blue tendrils of smoke here and there, the acrid fumes competing with clouds of Poison and Opium and Calvin Klein.

A tinny burst of laughter attracted Finny's attention. Hilarity reigned between the two couples who could have been fulfilling an acting class exercise: Sleek Young Couples Cavort. "Oh, Timmy, you're so single-mindedly *wicked.*" The feather-haired brunette pouted enchantingly at her escort.

Timmy exchanged a man-to-man glance with his tall friend who was braced against the body of an anorexic blonde in a metallic blue dress that clung as tightly as she did.

The nearly floor-to-ceiling Cubist painting behind them observed their antics with geometric calm. Finny's mouth curved in a sympathetic smile until she caught the angled, phallic representation Timmy was pointing to and heard the snickers of his friends.

A few feet away, a photographer snapped a shot of their self-conscious enjoyment, and Finny winced at the flash of light. The man lowered his camera, his jutting eyebrows aslant over deep-set eyes filled with contempt.

Finny moved on. If she hadn't agreed to get a drink for Cuffy she'd find Chris and get out of here. Her eyes caught the flutter of Twee's fingers waving at her from across the room where she loomed over a slender man in white. Finny waved back tepidly. Surely Twee would consider her good deed done by now.

She crested the marble steps, glanced around, saw Barelli standing at the bar beside a short, redheaded woman. He saw her as she approached and said something to the redhead, who turned toward Finny, her hair swirling about her shoulders, her deep green dress draping gracefully over a knockout figure.

"So, you're the guest of honor tonight. I had wondered." The sultriness of her voice was enough to change Colorado's semiarid climate into a tropical zone.

"This is Abigail Hunter," Barelli said. "She's the society reporter for the *Post*, so watch what you say."

"You can't be that hard-up for quotes." Finny put the glasses on the bar with a quiet word to the bartender. "It's nice to meet you. I'm surprised you'd cover something like this."

Abigail Hunter laughed lightly. "You know Twee. She was determined to go all out, and it was unusual enough for me to drop in."

"I suppose so." Finny glanced around at the noisy room. "Twee must've invited almost everybody she's ever known."

"No, just the important ones." Abigail's shadowed eyes narrowed a little. "What kind of relationship do you two have anyway?"

"We're friends. Why?"

The shiny green material of her gown shimmered as Abigail shrugged. "Just that I would've sworn that nothing less than blackmail would have gotten some of these people to show up. Twee does love to step on people's toes and make them like it."

Finny picked up the full champagne glasses from the bar. "You couldn't prove it by me," she said. "Unless you think Twee's using me to step on those toes. Or she blackmailed you to show up."

Abigail shook her head a little at the dry note in Finny's voice. "Now don't misunderstand me. Twee's a love, a real oasis on the scene. I was just curious."

"An occupational hazard, I'm sure." Finny looked past her at Barelli. "I need to deliver this and then I'm ready to go. How about you?"

"Sure."

Finny left Barelli and Abigail to brave the crush once more. She finally caught sight of Cuffy's copper hair.

"Excuse me." Finny eased her way between two men attempting to pass as CPAs. "Take one of these before I do any more damage," she told Cuffy, extending a glass.

Cuffy took it. "I was beginning to think you'd—" The mischievous smile disappeared, and her gaze fixed painfully on something behind Finny.

Finny turned to look behind her.

"How long have you been here?" Kit Landauer's sapphire eyes were electric with anger. "I didn't see you come in."

Cuffy shrugged and lifted her glass to her mouth. The faint trembling of her hand disturbed the bubbling surface of the champagne. "There's no reason why you should have," she said in a colorless voice.

"Damn it, Cuffy, you promised you'd let me know when you—"

"I never promised you anything." Cuffy shot him a quick look of defiance. "You *assumed* something that wasn't true, just as you always do."

"Wait just a damned minute," Kit began hotly.

"For God's sake, lower your voice." Cuffy slanted a look at Finny. "I'm sorry. Kit and I have some unfinished business. Would you excuse us?"

"Certainly." Finny turned to go and slammed into the ruffled front of Twee Garrett. Her champagne sloshed over one side of her glass.

"Here you are." Twee grabbed her shoulders and turned her toward the sea of souls whence she'd sprung. Finny glanced behind her in time to see Kit Landauer take hold of Cuffy's wrist.

"I've had former Commissioner Nielsson trapped for ten minutes, talking about the trophy cases he wants built in his den. He shoots skeet, you know." One hand pushed firmly at the small of Finny's back, the other waving gaily at a bald, unsmiling man forging his way away from the refreshment table. "My lawyer; a lovely man." She prodded Finny again. "Get going; the commissioner won't keep for long. He's shockingly forgetful."

"Twee." Finny craned her neck round. Twee looked grim with determination, pale with a fine misting of perspiration on her forehead, her lips tight with resolve. "I think it's about time I went home."

"Don't be silly, darling. You haven't met everyone yet. Don't forget, the whole party's for you."

"Yeah, but if I don't get some rest, I won't be able to follow up on all these opportunities." Finny stopped and turned. "I'm serious, Twee. I have to get up at six."

Concern swamped Twee's soft features. "Oh, my dear, I had no idea. You should have told me. I could have set—"

The crash of glassware and metal once again split through the wall-to-wall noise.

"Oh, heavens," moaned Twee, "if that's the new girl *again*—"

A blood-curdling scream drowned out her words.

Four

"GOOD MORNING, Denver, Big Chuck Harroldson here on this gorgeous Colorado day! Welcome to KGBY's 'Speak Out,' where the listener rules the airwaves. What's on your mind this bright Monday morning, Denver? Give me a call at 999-TALK. And we have Genevieve on line one. Good morning, Genevieve, you're on the air."

"Hello, Chuck? I think you're just great, and I want you to know that everybody in my neighborhood never misses your show."

"Well, thanks, Genevieve, and what's on your mind this morning?"

"Chuck, I think that judge that got killed last night, you know, the one that's in this morning's paper? Well, I don't like to speak ill of the dead, but I think he got what's coming to him, you know? He let several bad people go free or just as near as, and I think that it was like a judgment of God that he himself was struck down—"

The pillow that covered Finny's head moved convulsively as she flailed at the clock radio with one hand. She connected with the alarm switch and the querulous voice died.

"Oh, God." Finny's eyes opened far enough to see the golden edging around the window blinds. She hadn't switched off the alarm. Which made it six in the A.M. Which meant she'd had three hours' sleep. And Corinne Danovich was waiting for her new linen cupboard.

By the time Finny was out of the shower, Barelli had made it home. He was sitting on the bed, his face reflect-

23

ing all of his forty-four years: bleary-eyed, mouth tight with fatigue, dark hair falling every which way. His crumpled suit jacket covered shoulders slumped in weariness.

Finny crossed the room and stood in front of him. Their eyes met for a blank moment, and then her hand was stroking the back of his neck, his head bent against her. "You look like hell."

"Can't look as bad as I feel." His voice was rough. "Last night was like paint remover—industrial strength—on the old, thin veneer of civilization. I've been in riots that were more fun."

He was shrugging out of his coat and she helped him pull it over his shoulders and down his arms. "After you left, we still had half a dozen of the party guests to talk to. Their lawyers loved that. *They* swarmed in like wasps as soon as the word got out. Not to mention the guests who were lawyers themselves. Then there was the press." He rubbed both hands over his face. "Put a bunch of lawyers up against reporters and you can sell even a pacifist on the neutron bomb."

Finny was unbuttoning his shirt. "How long before you have to go back?"

"Not long enough." He yawned and shook his head. "I'm s'posed to be back at noon." He lay back onto the rumpled sheets, his shirt open. "Gotta interview Landauer—he wouldn't say diddly without his mouthpiece—and some old bat who was screeching like a goosed nun, and good ol' Twee's lawyer wants to talk again . . ." His voice trailed off.

Finny tugged the light bedspread out from under him and pulled it up over his long legs. She lifted his head gently and pushed a pillow under it.

"Mmmmm-hmmmm." Barelli nestled into the cool softness.

Finny pulled on jeans and a t-shirt and dug through a drawer for socks. Barelli murmured and shifted on the bed. She scooped up her running shoes and went downstairs.

The kitchen was starting to glow with the newly minted sunshine that beamed through the room's eastern window.

The greenhouse windows on the west side stared out at the yard, still filled with the lingering shadows that would shrink in dreamy increments as the day began.

Finny set her shoes on a wicker chair and plodded barefoot across cool tiles to the refrigerator. If she could mainline coffee—real, caffeine-laden coffee—she might get her eyelids at half-mast. The coffeemaking ritual was automatic, its movements as set as Kabuki theater. Finny poured the coffee into a cup and set the carafe back onto its hot plate. Her thoughts were drawn like iron filings to the magnet of Twee's party the night before.

The crash of crockery had been followed by a shrill scream that had killed the party babble as abruptly as a time whistle stops factory work, leaving silence in its wake. A broken voice sobbing "He's dead, he's dead," had jolted the crowded room into sound and motion, the shocked guests pushing at each other like cattle herded into pens, each demanding of the others, "What's *going on?*" Finny caught a quick glimpse of the maid, her dark face contorted in horror, her eyes trained on something at her feet.

Finny ran up to the edge of the crush. Beyond the gaping people, a young blond woman—the one in the black strapless gown, she realized—was on her knees amidst shattered dishes and scattered silverware. She was crying brokenly. Noting the vague motions of the woman's hand, Finny headed through the doorway to the hall that led to the kitchen, the mud room, and, ultimately the back door of the house. Behind her puffed Twee, making small, dismayed sounds.

The hallway was empty, and when she got to the kitchen, Finny saw that it was, too.

"Outside," she heard as she came back to the hall, now crowded with people shuffling toward the open door. She got behind Les Trethalwyn and let him run interference.

They came out into the night. The clear, starlit sky arched protectively over the scents of summer and the quiet lapping of the swimming pool's breeze-induced tide. The herd of guests moved over the deck, their feet striking drumbeats on the redwood surface, then suddenly stopping. Over Les's shoulder, Finny could see something lying on the flagstone apron of the pool, its nature hidden in the shadows cast by the murky light behind it.

She walked down the steps, around the people between her and the pool. "Who is it?" someone appealed. "What's happening?"

As Finny approached the crumpled figure, bright security lights at the corners of the house switched on. There was a gasp from behind her. Finny glanced over her shoulder and saw Paige Dexter, her face ghostly in the glare, her hands wrapped around one of Ty Engelman's arms as if around a lifeline.

When she first saw Judge Sarandon lying on the flagstone, she thought for one mad second there'd been a mistake. How stupid they all were going to feel, her mind flashed, when they realized he'd fainted and that the stain down his shirt and tie was the burgundy she'd made him spill. And then reality intruded. Even if grade-A wishful thinking could see burgundy instead of blood, it would take a damn sight more to transform the rosewood skewer handle protruding from Sarandon's chest into a tie tack.

"Oh, my God," Twee said in a high, little voice.

Finny ignored her and the jostling bodies behind her, moving forward to kneel beside the judge. The babble level went from low to high as she placed her fingertips on Sarandon's neck. She couldn't find a pulse.

Barelli shouldered his way through the human wall and squatted beside her. "Let me check," he said, and repeated Finny's actions. "Call the department," he said finally. "Tell them to send an ambulance."

Finny shot him a surprised glance.

"For the body," he said softly.

The noise level rose at his words. William Sarandon had met with a summary judgment and everybody wanted to talk about it.

Finny stood up and pushed her way through the people between her and the door. She looked for Cuffy, but she wasn't to be seen in the faces that now floated around the judge's body like helium-filled balloons. She heard Barelli's voice rising, ordering people to stand away from the body.

Then the evening slipped into illusory time and crept onward, its new markers the comings and goings of the police, the coroner's office people; the mixture of outrage and resignation as the party guests were herded and separated, identified and interviewed. Telephones rang and doorbells chimed with the thwarted efforts of reporters to pin down the sequence of events before their papers' deadlines or their morning news shows.

Finny was in the kitchen, curled up on the Brobdinagian rocking chair that nestled next to the cold, manor-sized fireplace when Twee found her. It was after midnight.

The hours had been unkind to Twee, breaching the armor of makeup, wilting her silver-and-black ruffles. A washboard of wrinkles creased her brow; her violet hair sagged alarmingly.

"You've got to talk to your lieutenant," she said forcefully. She loomed over Finny like a creature out of mythology. "He's simply got to let Cuffy and Paige go home."

Finny focused her eyes and struggled to understand. "What?"

"Your lieutenant won't let them leave—it isn't fair—they shouldn't have to put up with it."

"Christ, Twee." Finny rubbed at her eyes with both hands. "He's not out to torture anybody. He's trying to figure out who killed the judge."

"I know that." Twee's expression was wild, and tears were making distinct inroads at the corners. "But it's too much to expect her to stay here. Their separation was bitter, but that doesn't mean Paige isn't upset. And Cuffy's just gone all quiet, as if she isn't even here."

The words rattled around inside Finny's head for a few seconds before they shaped themselves into coherence. "Separation? Whose?"

"William's and Paige's, of course." Twee's mouth trembled. "Just because their marriage didn't survive doesn't make Paige not care about his murder. She's not a robot, you know."

"Paige Dexter was married to Judge Sarandon?" Finny stared at Twee glassily, half wondering if she was hearing right. "You mean she's Cuffy's—"

"Mother. Of course, Cuffy's stronger than Paige, much stronger, but she's close to the edge, too. This is such a shock—"

"You're telling me!" Finny shook her head. "Why does Paige have a different name—Dexter instead of Sarandon?"

"She never did use William's name in public," Twee said numbly. "She had her own identity before she was married. Paige was always the 'little Dexter princess.'" Anger came into her expression. "What difference does it make? Will you talk to your policeman friend?"

Finny raised one hand. "Okay. I'll see what I can do." She pushed herself up out of the chair. "Where's Chris now?"

"The family room." Twee pressed the handkerchief she clutched in one hand against her lips. "Family room. What a stupid name for a room . . . Just Herbert and I—oh God, I wish he was here." Her voice quavered.

Finny paused, then put her arms around Twee, felt the trembling that rippled through her. "This must be so horrible for you, Twee. I'm sorry that it had to happen here."

Twee pulled out of her hold and pressed the scrap of cloth against one eye, then the other. "Just help get it over with. You can do that, can't you? Your lieutenant will listen, won't he?"

"I'll see."

"Just do it, Finny." The choked words had the ring of command. "Do it for me."

Finny nodded.

The silence of the living room was stark in contrast to its earlier hubbub. The paintings and sculptures housed in the huge area seemed otherworldly in such emptiness, their messages lost in the absence of witnesses. The click of Finny's heels on the marble floor was slowly drowned in the sound of the voices that flowed from the arched doorway off the far end of the room.

Les Trethalwyn came out the door, nearly colliding with

Finny. He reached automatically to steady her. His face was pasty, his eyes shadowed with the horror of the night's events. "Are you all right?"

"Yes. How about you?"

"God, this has been a nightmare." He rubbed one hand across his mouth, long fingers trembling. "I could do with a drink, a very large drink, anywhere that isn't here. D'you want to come with me?"

For a moment Finny wanted to go. "Thanks, but I'd better not."

"Then I'll be seeing you." He walked past her, his pace increasing with each step.

Finny paused as she entered Twee's family room. If the more public part of the house had all the ambience of an art gallery, Twee had made up for it in this place. Thick tweed carpet and knotty pine paneling warmed the air. A well-used gray sofa was dotted by soft, multicolored pillows. A hulking captain's desk provided the only interruption in the banks of shelves that extended across one wall, all of them laden with books and magazines. A huge television screen was the centerpiece of the wall opposite the shelves, and several bright orange Broncos pennants had been tacked above it. Two recliners held pride of place near the TV, one accompanied by an end table inundated with books and newspapers, the other holding an enormous Teddy bear who stared fixedly at the TV set.

Barelli was propped against the bar at the far end of the room, a telephone receiver squeezed between his neck and shoulder. He'd loosened his tie and unbuttoned his shirt collar. His eyes met Finny's briefly and then moved away as his conversation intensified.

Eddie Apodaca, Barelli's partner, was in quiet conversation with one of the party's three-piece suits, a pale young man whose moist eyes were framed in heavy tortoiseshell glasses that he removed and replaced in punctuation to his nervous tenor voice. Eddie was his usual camouflaged self, in a dark, I'm-just-a-civil-servant suit, white button-down shirt, and measured stripe tie. Under the close-cropped black hair, graying in spots, creases were lining up on his forehead and his fleshy nose was pinched in at the corners. Impatience looked out of weary eyes cushioned by dark circles.

"Excuse me." Finny was pushed aside by a whirlwind in green who strode across the room toward Barelli. Abigail Hunter's thick red hair rose and settled on her shoulders with each determined step. She charged with all the subtlety of a tank across the room's thick carpeting.

"Lieutenant." Her voice was steely.

Barelli nodded to her, then returned to his telephone conversation.

"Lieutenant." More loudly.

Barelli put a hand over the receiver and looked down his straight, sharp nose at her, his eyes narrowed.

"One of your henchmen told me that I wasn't allowed to make a phone call. Is that true?"

"That's right, Miss Hunter. No calls yet."

Her pale hands, each finger tipped in red nail polish, rested on her hips. "That's unconstitutional."

"Bullshit." He shifted in irritation. "Look, you'll get your story out. I just don't want you doing it yet. You'll have to excuse me." He put the receiver back to his ear.

Abigail's eyes widened in shock. "I'll see that your superiors hear about this, Lieutenant," she stormed. "After all the trouble the chief has gone to to improve the PD's public image, he'll have your head for lunch."

"He doesn't eat Italian." Barelli turned his shoulder to her.

"You bastard. I won't forget this." She whirled around and stalked back across the room. Eyes flashing, nostrils flared, she was magnificently angry.

She spared Finny a glance, cocked her nose a little higher, charged through the door. Where the hell did she get that kind of energy this time of night, Finny wondered sourly.

Barelli hung up the phone and ambled across the room in Fury's wake. "How you doin', babe? You look done in."

"Thanks." She motioned toward the door. "Dear old Abigail seems a little put out."

"She wants to get a jump on her Pulitzer." Barelli's

wide mouth stretched in a smile. " 'I Was There,' and all that."

"Why do I believe that she's not going to mention you in kindly terms?"

Barelli put one arm around her shoulders and moved her toward the bar. "Who gives a damn? She's been hanging out with the polo players too long. Thinks she's one of 'em." He pulled a bar stool out and pushed her onto it. "I was about to go looking for you. You ready to be grilled?"

"I'm ready to go to bed." Finny let her head rest on one hand. "Grilled about what?"

"Anything you saw, anybody you talked to that might have something to do with this mess."

"Oh, you're ready to hear from the pro, eh?"

He snagged another stool and sat down beside her. "Hell yes, baby, tell me all you know."

Finny gave him a rapid, precise summary of her trial by wine with the judge; the interrupted conversation with Cuffy, including the tension between her and Kit Landauer; and what she'd observed of Paige Dexter, primarily the interest she'd taken in Ty Engelman.

"When I heard the scream—who was that, anyway? The maid or the blond woman?"

"The blonde," Barelli said. "Name of Simms Bainbridge. She stumbled over Sarandon and ran back into the house. Slam bang into the maid."

"You sure *she* didn't kill him?"

Barelli shrugged tiredly. "As sure as I am of anything. According to her and the guy with the accent, she went out for a little slap and tickle with him."

"You mean the guy who just left? Les Trethalwyn?"

"Yeah. So," he added, "tell me what you know."

"I was with Twee," Finny began. "She followed me outside and I was behind Les Trethalwyn. I saw Ty and Paige out there; they were behind me." She paused. "Let's see, I've met only about a million people tonight, so the names are fuzzy. I know that the little gray man that Twee was talking to when I saw you at the bar was near the front of the crowd."

"Former Commissioner Nielsson." Barelli eyed her with respect. "Have you figured out who did it yet?"

Finny scowled at him. "No, but if I were a betting woman, I'd put my money on Paige Dexter."

"Why?"

"Because she's a bitch on wheels and it's always so satisfying to put that type away."

"Damned courts want more than that to convict." Barelli stood up and rolled his shoulders. "You want me to get somebody to drive you home?"

"How long are you going to be?" Finny stretched her jaws in a yawn.

"God knows. Probably it'll be dawn's early light by the time we talk to everybody at least once."

Finny's eyes moved around the room. "Everybody who?"

Barelli sighed. "Cleary's got a bunch down in the basement area. The 'mother-in-law apartment' is what some real estate type called it. Want some coffee? There's some down there."

She shook her head. "I suppose you need the car." At his nod she yawned. "I think I'll take that ride. I'm supposed to build a linen cabinet tomorrow." She leaned briefly into his hand as it cupped her cheek.

"I'll be right back." He started to turn away, then stopped at her hand on his arm.

"Twee wanted me to work my wiles on you. She thinks you ought to let Paige Dexter go home since she and Sarandon were married."

"I just did," Barelli said. "She and her daughter left a few minutes ago."

"I like Cuffy. I never did get a chance to tell her how sorry I am." Finny shook her head. "What a way to have your father check out. She was already upset at the kind of publicity he was getting after the Parmetter case."

"Yeah."

At the flatness in his voice, Finny raised her head and looked at him. "We were talking to each other nearly the whole time her father was supposedly cleaning off the wine I spilled all over him."

"Come on, Finny, you know how the game is played. I can't talk about any of this right now."

"She's a good kid, Chris."

"Uh-huh." He pulled her off the stool by one hand. "Come on, let's get you that ride."

One of the patrolmen had brought her home, saying little, and she had tumbled into bed as the clock was chiming two. Who could find it unusual if the thought of the evening's entertainment had kept her awake until three or so?

The faces had floated through her mind each time she'd shut her eyes. The anxiety in Cuffy's face when they'd talked about the notoriety that came with being her father's daughter; the charge in the air when Paige Dexter had greeted Ty Engelman; the trouble that aged Twee Garrett's indomitable countenance. Hell and damn, and the party had been for her.

Finny slapped together a peanut butter and jelly sandwich to eat while she drove to work and grabbed the thermos that had drained upside down in the dish rack by the sink. She filled it with coffee, twisted the stopper tightly, and set it on the counter. She pulled out a carton of yogurt and an apple and put them in a sack. She would go to work and build a lovely, graceful cabinet for Corinne Danovich. That, at least, was something she could do.

It was Barelli's job to sift through the snarled threads of motive and opportunity. He and Eddie and the others would reach a conclusion and that would finish it. Justice would triumph and a new cabinet would hold treasured linens. God would be in his heav'n. And William Sarandon would still be dead.

Finny picked up her lunch and tucked the thermos under one arm, grabbing her handbag on the way out, pulling the door shut behind her. Her pickup started on the first try and she backed it out into the alley. The sun was bright on the quiet streets. A dog barked down the block. She pointed herself in the direction of the Danovich three-story dinosaur on the West Side.

Finny drove toward the mountains. Tired and sad, she was unable to erase the troubled faces from her mind.

Five

THE SHINING TEETH of the saw blade sliced through birch molding. Finny turned off the saw and set it down on the floor. When she blew the sawdust off the cut end, the clean, sharp scent of the wood rested on the air like sunshine.

She whistled absently between her teeth as she climbed up the stepladder until she could reach the top edge of the linen cabinet. Roughly triangular in shape, the cabinet nestled in the northwest corner of the second-story hallway that connected the four bedrooms originally built for the daughters of Arnold Kenston, an early mercantile force in Denver's history. According to Corinne Danovich, the present owner of the house, at least one of Arnold's daughters had fully shared her father's interest in economic issues, with herself as primary commodity.

Finny traced around the edge of the back molding with a pencil, then descended the ladder. She rummaged among her tools for her coping saw, then carefully cut along the light mark. The crown molding along the top edge of the cabinet repeated a pattern used throughout the house, particularly in the butler's pantry off the kitchen.

She was done drilling nail holes in the molding when Corinne's reedy voice drifted up from downstairs. "There's a phone call for you, Finny."

"I'll be right down."

The worn Oriental runner moved under her feet on several steps as she pounded downstairs, and Finny made a mental note to tack it down.

"It's a man. He didn't say who," Corinne murmured as Finny came into the kitchen. She was slicing up a chicken at the slate counter, her small, lined face atwitch with curiosity.

Finny nodded and picked up the receiver. "Finny Aletter."

"You'd better sit down, sweetheart." Barelli was definitely awake and edgy, judging by the crispness in his voice. "Twee Garrett's confessed to killing William Sarandon."

"What?" At the shocked sound, Corinne turned toward her.

"She and her lawyer came in about an hour ago."

"You've got to be kidding." Finny's mind was swirling with images from the night before. "Dammit, Chris, there's no way—*I don't believe it.*"

"Take it easy. It's a little hard for me to swallow, too. Just a minute." Barelli had put his hand over the receiver, Finny concluded from the muffled noises in her ear. Then he was back. "The DA's office is falling all over itself. Johnny Seavers wasn't looking forward to our investigation of the country club set."

"But why, Chris? Why? What possible reason could she have had?"

"Evidently Judge Sarandon did dirt to Herbert Garrett some years back. Pulled out of a business deal that put Garrett in deep shit without hip boots, according to Twee. Seavers is smiling so big his gums are sunburned."

"That's bullshit, Chris. Twee would have a hard time stepping on a spider, unless one of her pet causes were involved."

"How much of a pet was old Herbert?"

Corinne was keeping her eyes carefully on the knife slicing through gristle, her narrow shoulders square with the effort at nonchalance. Finny turned her back and lowered her voice. "Revenge on the grand scale? Number one: she's about as likely a killer as Winnie the Pooh; number two: if she decided to commit murder, she damn well wouldn't do it at a party in her own home. She's not stupid or crazy, Chris."

"Well, not stupid. I don't like the feel of it either, babe, but Seavers likes his presents wrapped and tied with a bow. Twee gave him this one and then unwrapped it for him."

"Yeah, but wait a minute. I was there, remember?" Finny was thinking feverishly. "Twee and I split up when I ran away to hit the rest room. Then I talked to Ty and Paige came over."

"Finny—"

"Just a minute. Ty took about five to ten minutes. Then I ran into the judge. He chewed me out—that was about five minutes—and he left to get cleaned up. Cuffy and I talked."

"I gotta go—"

Finny's voice had slipped into retrospective abstraction. "I saw Twee when I went to the bar for refills. You were talking to Abigail Hunter. I took the drinks back, Kit showed up. Let's see, Twee ambushed me right after that. She'd been talking to Commissioner Whatsis. . . . When the hell could she have killed Sarandon? There wasn't any time, Chris. I'm almost sure of it."

Barelli's voice was impatient. "But why would she say she had if she didn't?"

"Why would she say she did if she did?" Finny countered swiftly.

"I don't know." He was sounding harried. "Can't talk anymore, gotta go."

At a thump from the counter, Finny glanced over in time to see Corinne halve the chicken carcass with a small cleaver. "Chris, what about physical evidence? Fingerprints, all the Sherlock stuff?"

"The skewer was wiped, there was nothing on the body, and, given the seventeen thousand footprints around the scene, we were surprised Sarandon died of a stab wound. I've got to go."

"Wait. What about dinner?"

"Looks like a strong maybe. If I can't make it, I'll call. And I put a chicken in the Crockpot."

"Swell." Finny averted her eyes from Corinne's efficient disassembly of her poultry victim.

"I know this is tough for you. We'll talk more tonight. 'Bye."

Finny replaced the receiver.

"Is there a problem?" Corinne's milky blue eyes glimmered with curiosity. Her age-spotted hands had stilled on the pile of chicken parts.

"Hmmm? Oh, no. No problem." Finny positioned the plain black telephone back in the center of its shelf. "I may have to stop a little early today. I've got some business to take care of."

"Whatever you need to do." Corinne glanced down at her hands and began dropping pieces of chicken into a paper bag. She was a perfect accessory to the lovingly restored kitchen: gray hair in a sparse coronet, wearing a flowered housedress with a white apron and her narrow feet in no-nonsense black-laced Etta Jennicks. Her face was lined with fine tributaries etched by numerous go-rounds with experience. "I read about the judge's death." She glanced at Finny from the corners of eyes that were snapping with interest. "The morning paper said the party was for you."

"Did it?" God, here we go again, Finny thought. It hadn't occurred to her to check.

"That society writer had a whole big piece on it."

"Could I take a look?" Tomorrow's headlines would make Abigail Hunter's story look like an Easter egg roll.

Corinne was already wiping off her hands on a terry dishtowel. "Of course. Just let me find it." She scrabbled through the neat stack of papers on the sideboard, retrieving the relevant section with a little crow of triumph. "Here it is."

Finny barely glanced at the formal head shot of William Sarandon that was displayed beside a headline in thirty-six-point type. Her eyes were skimming the article under Abigail's boldface byline.

" '—stabbed with a skewer near the heart through his silk Gucci tie,' " Finny read aloud, subsiding into a mutter. " 'His controversial decision in the Parmetter case was cited by several sources as a possible motive . . . When we're ready for the press to know something, we'll tell them,' said Denver Police Lieutenant Christopher Barelli, severe in an off-the-rack gray suit." Finny threw down the paper in disgust. "Bitch. She said she'd get him."

She retrieved the newspaper, absently folding the sheets before replacing them on the table. The whole thing was fantastic. Twee was probably capable of killing. Most people were if the right buttons got pushed. But it seemed an awfully long time between "push" and "shove." One thing was certain, though: Twee was fiercely partisan—witness her determination to help Finny in her new career, and her belief in the goodwill of Paige Dexter (speaking of bitches), and she had been determinedly protective of Paige and Cuffy last night. How far would she go for the people she loved?

"Corinne, I do need to leave," Finny said suddenly. "I'll be back in the morning."

Finny couldn't get in to see Twee. She'd raced home, assumed professional camouflage with her most conservative business suit, white silk shirt and all, and braved the elegant fortress that was the Denver Police Administration building.

The young policewoman at the reception desk in the lobby, unmoved by her sartorial splendor, was polite but firm. "I'm sorry, Miss Aletter, but it's impossible. The only people who can see Mrs. Garrett are her lawyer and representatives of the DA's office. No exceptions."

Barelli wasn't in and Eddie Apodaca wasn't riding a white charger when he came down from Homicide to the cavernous first floor to talk with her. His brown eyes danced in genuine amusement when she asked him to help her get to Twee.

"Un-unh, Finny. No way, no how. This little case is hands-off territory. The DA's office is runnin' it tighter than a Gestapo fire drill."

"Eddie, it's important that I talk to her."

"Sorry, no can do."

"Thanks," she said dispiritedly. She jammed her fists into her jacket pockets and turned away. Then she remembered what the officer in reception had said, and turned back. "Eddie, hold it." He stopped on his way to the elevator and waited while she crossed the floor. "If I get permission from her lawyer can I see her?"

"I don't know. Maybe."

"Where do I find out who's representing her?"

Eddie wasn't smiling as he pulled a pen from his pale yellow shirt pocket. "You gotta promise no tricks."

"Huh?"

"Don't 'huh' me," he said grimly. "Chris may've forgot some of the stunts you pulled when Elliot Fulton was killed, but I got a longer memory. Promise."

Finny crossed her heart, then glanced into Eddie's eyes and got serious. "I promise. Look, I just think something weird is going on here—"

"I definitely do not want to know. Stay here a minute." Eddie walked quickly to the reception desk and spoke in a low voice to the officer behind it. She handed him the phone receiver. He was back in a couple of minutes.

"Here's her lawyer's name, and his address. Do me a favor: forget where you got it."

"Thanks, Eddie. I appreciate it."

"Yeah? Then remember your promise."

The address had brought Finny to the Denver Tech Center, a mixed architectural bag of metal and glass structures that had sprung up on either side of I-25 like mechanistic mushrooms among the southward crawl of suburban housing developments. The offices of Bartholomew, Erickson, and Fannlowe, Attorneys-at-Law, were nestled in a building that, if supplied with booster rockets, could have spurred a whole new rash of UFO citings. Its sheets of copper-colored glass reflected the bright afternoon light, a manmade sun shining its heat on rows of fast-food restaurants crouched waiting at the edges of the capillary network of streets and overpasses that radiated from the highway like split ends on a bad hairdo.

After a forty-five-minute wait overseen by an angular, young blond woman who looked more suited to a hockey field than to the anonymous, plush furnishings of the reception area, Finny had been admitted into the inner sanctum of Twee's lawyer. And no further.

"Miss Aletter, I haven't time to indulge in fruitless conversation." MacKenzie Bartholomew's face was closed tighter than a childproof medicine bottle. "Mrs. Garrett gave me specific instructions. She refuses to see anyone except for *myself*. As her attorney, I must respect her wishes."

"Wrong. As her attorney you must act in her best interests." Finny pushed herself out of the overstuffed leather chair that threatened to swallow her. She leaned against the front edge of Bartholomew's desk, a slab of black urethane big enough to go undercover as a parking lot. "Can you honestly tell me that you believe Twee killed William Sarandon?"

"I can't honestly tell you anything," Bartholomew said precisely. "Nor will I." His bald head reflected the light of the fluorescent panels recessed in the ceiling, and his small, pale eyes glittered at her under ferocious gray eyebrows. "If that's all, Miss Aletter . . ."

Finny's fist struck the desktop. "Goddamn it, you were there last night! Didn't you see her? She didn't have time to kill Sarandon and I think I can prove it. Not only is Twee screwing herself, she's keeping the police from looking for the real murderer."

Bartholomew pushed his dimpled swivel chair away from his desk and stood up. His three-piece blue pinstripe suit rearranged itself gracefully to accommodate the new position. "I suppose you think you're acting as a friend. Let me assure you that this is none of your business. I suggest you busy yourself with something else." He came around the desk. "I'll see you out." His hand closed around her arm with unexpected strength, and he urged her through the door, conducting her to the outer office.

"Miss Scranton, Miss Aletter was just leaving. If she has any difficulty finding her way out, please call the security guard to help her." Without taking further notice of Finny, he went back into his office and closed the door.

TRIP WIRE

SHE WALKED past the Westwood housing project, pretending she didn't hear the child screaming from one window open on the street side. The square, boxy redbrick buildings of the project were punctuated with blue-trimmed doors and windows. The paint had been applied with care—there were no splotches on the windows—but the buildings were tired and an air of defeat clung to them as surely as the heat clung to the air.

Three children chased another child across grass drying in the day's summer fire, one shrieking, "I'll fucking kill you, asshole. You don't deal straight with me, you fucking die." The two little girls running beside him giggled, one chiming in, "You asshole."

Without Miguel she would have to try to get into a place like this one. If she could, which wasn't likely.

Traffic noise penetrated in a hot, heavy stream from Federal Boulevard, where she'd left the bus, through the three-block buffer of bustling Southeast Asian restaurants and markets, past mom-and-pop businesses and auto parts stores. A siren slashed through the stampede of cars and trucks, their horns blaring like animal cries, and answering howls went up from dogs all over the neighborhood.

Bianca stumbled as she went up the concrete steps to the door of the dishwater-gray frame house. Her key stuck in the lock and she had to work it a little to get it to draw back the deadbolt. Miguel had installed the lock after the break-in five months before.

The living room was heavy with heat, sun beaming through the venetian blinds, the rays laden with dust motes floating listlessly like dead ideas. She dropped her tote bag on the worn, maroon studio couch and headed for the kitchen.

She would wash her uniform later. If she hung it in the bathroom, it would dry easily in two hours.

The tiny kitchen still reeked of the bacon she'd fried that morning to leave for Miguel. He'd slept through the small sounds she'd made getting ready for work. He'd held her until early in the morning, trying to soothe her, telling her the police wouldn't find out, wouldn't arrest her and send her back.

The ring of the telephone clamored through the weighted air and spurred her heart into double time. She waited until it rang again, then lifted the receiver to her ear. "Hello?"

"Jita, how'd it go?"

She leaned against the kitchen counter. "Okay. I think. *La policia* left before lunch. *Senora* Garrett, she goes out in the afternoon and doesn't come back."

"Did the cops bother you?"

"No, they ask for coffee, that's all."

Miguel's voice eased into its usual light tone. "You see, I told you. You're nothing to them, just part of the scenery."

"Maybe." She paused, then spoke quickly. "Miguel, before she goes, Senora Garrett is *muy agitato* and she is crying to Senor Bartholomew. He yells back, he is *mas loco que una cabra."*

"Why was he so mad at her?"

"No sabo."

"Damn." He was silent for a moment, then spoke slowly. "All right. Just do what you normally do. Go to work, don't ask any questions. And don't be afraid. They're not going to notice you, *jita,* unless you make them. *Comprende?"*

"Si."

"Good. I'll be there as soon as I can."

"You'll be late?"

"That wedding, remember?" His voice was

soothing again. "I'll take the pictures, then I'll be home. You just sit tight, okay?"

"Okay, Miguel." She held the receiver after he hung up, wishing she didn't feel so afraid.

Six

THE MEMORY of MacKenzie Bartholomew's stonewalling still rankled over dinner. Finny barely tasted the chicken cacciatore that Barelli had fixed. "It was the smoothest bum's rush I ever got." She pushed a thigh bone to one side of her plate with her fork. "I might as well have tried to crash the mint."

"He was right; it isn't any of your business." Barelli picked up the wine bottle. "You want any more?"

Finny pushed her glass toward him. "What kind of lawyer will let his client confess to a murder?"

"Usually one who hopes to cut as good a deal as possible with the DA, meaning that his client's chances are roughly comparable to hell's own snowball." Barelli poured too fast and cursed under his breath as the wine splashed out of her glass. He wiped up the spill with an abrupt swipe of his napkin. "What makes you so damned sure she didn't do it?"

"You met her." Finny put down her knife and fork. "I've known her for years, and in all that time I've never known her to deliberately hurt anybody. How many people can you say that about?" She pushed back her chair and stood up. "No matter how I try, I can't see her committing murder. That's the bottom line, Chris. Besides, I still think she didn't have time." She picked up their dinner plates and carried them to the counter. "I don't know what she's up to, but I've got a feeling . . ."

Barelli got up from the table. He made a reflex gesture toward the pocket of his green t-shirt, then dropped his hand to the pocket of his faded jeans for a roll of Lifesavers buried there. Quitting smoking hadn't been easy for him. "If you're going to talk intuition—"

Finny scraped a plate viciously. "So help me, if you say one sexist word about women's intuition, I'll—"

"You'll what?" Barelli came up behind her, reached past her to turn off the faucet. "Gut feelings get no argument from me. Half my job involves hunches." He turned her around so that he could see her face. Water dripped from her hands onto her legs, bared by the cutoffs she wore. Her brown eyes were troubled under the frowning black brows that were as dramatic against her sunburned forehead as Chinese letters on parchment.

Her lips were soft under his short, hard kiss. "What else have you got?" he challenged softly. "Hunches, gut feelings, even good old women's intuition will take you only so far. Then you've got to have the hard facts to back 'em up, babe."

"Right." Finny pulled out of his arms and tore off a paper towel from the roll to wipe off the drops of water scurrying down her legs. "And what I've got after today is nothing. I thought if I could talk to Twee I'd figure out what she's up to."

"So you ran into some brick walls. Now what?"

"I don't know." Finny picked up their full glasses from the table and went through the swinging door into the dining room, then through the archway to the living room and the big, brown corduroy couch. "Theorize? Guess?" She set the glasses on the coffee table and plopped onto the sofa.

The cushions gave a little under Barelli's weight as he sat down beside her. He handed her glass over and she leaned against the armrest, propping her legs across his lap.

"What drives me wild is the size of the party last night. There must have been a hundred people there."

"We counted seventy-three." Barelli took a sip of wine. "It was wall-to-wall."

"And any one of them could've killed Sarandon."

"Maybe. Given the opportunity and a modicum of good taste."

His voice was serious. He drank the rest of his wine and leaned forward to set his glass on the table. He glanced at her, read the assessment in her eyes. "Well?"

"You sound like you really hated him."

"He was an asshole. Judges like him make my job a hell of a lot harder than it has to be."

"The Parmetter case?"

"That's just the latest in a roll." He patted at his shirt pocket. "Shit. Sarandon never could figure out which side to come down on. Remember the Billy Houghton case? Couple of years ago? Guy beats a seventeen-year-old boy half to death and Sarandon sentences the son-of-a-bitch to the max—everything except pillory in the Civic Center—gives a blood-'n-guts sentencing speech that has the whole courtroom ready to lynch the guy. His lawyer files an appeal—undue influence on the jury, biased management of the case, looking cross-eyed at the defense—you name it. Houghton gets a new trial and everybody tiptoes through it after the first disaster. Houghton was out on the streets in less than two years. He killed a social worker ten days after he got out."

"God, Chris."

"Sarandon was a lousy lawyer and a worse judge. He never could decide if he was Roy Bean or Dear Abby—balls out or a slap on the wrist. He drove us crazy."

"How'd he get appointed?"

"Probably the usual political nod after mucho contributions to the dear old party, I can't remember which one. Not that it matters. Rumor has it that the governor's been trying to get him to resign for the last two years."

"Poor Cuffy."

Chris looked at her. "What do you mean?"

"Oh, she was pretty defensive about the Parmetter case. Guilt by association."

Barelli relaxed more deeply into the sofa cushions. "It wouldn't be easy being his kid. Although I suppose wealth softened the blow."

Finny raised a brow. "From being a judge?"

"From having money up the wazoo. The source of the contributions, don't you know." His eyes closed, and he looked as if a nap wasn't far off. "By the way," he said after a few moments, "some of that money came out of a partnership with Herbert Garrett."

"Hmmmm." Finny drank more of her wine, thinking. "But Twee isn't the only person who might have been interested in killing him."

"Not by a long shot." Barelli lifted her legs off his and levered his way out of the sofa. "You want some more wine?"

"Yeah. Bring the bottle." Finny leaned back against the sofa arm. The evening air was beginning to cool as the sun neared the Front Range; the haunting scent of honeysuckle whispered in with a breeze through the side window. The sheer lacy curtain waved like a spiderweb in the movement of the air.

Barelli had described the judge. What was the man like? The William Sarandon she'd met had seemed rigid and humorless. Hadn't Cuffy said that he took pride in his manners? Although he certainly wasn't demonstrating them last night. He acted as if she'd deliberately set out to harm him. He'd been as edgy as a convention of razor blades.

"Scoot over." Barelli slipped back beneath her legs and filled her glass. "You look thoughtful enough. Come up with anything?"

"Oh, hell, yes. Got it solved already. Had to be suicide."

"Brilliant. What's your proof?"

"He had good enough taste to find himself offensive. Q.E.D."

"Never could stand their shoes." Barelli rested his head on the sofa back. "Come on, what're you thinking about?"

Finny rubbed an index finger around the edge of the wineglass. It didn't hum. "Eddie said today that you'd forgotten the 'tricks' I pulled when Elliot died."

Barelli turned his head to look at her. "Tricks? You?"

"Did you?"

"Forget? No."

Finny looked at the red liquid in her glass. The deep color glowed with the back lighting from the window. "I never thought of what I did as trickery." Her gaze lifted to meet his eyes.

"You were doing what you had to do."

"Yes. It was a question of what the right thing was."

"I know that. Eddie does, too, or he would if he stopped to think about it. He tends to mother-hen me sometimes."

"He's still afraid you'll retire and he'll have to break in somebody else."

Barelli chuckled. "That's not so far from the truth."

The short silence between them was broken by the distant sound of siren.

Finny rubbed at the beginnings of an itch on one knee. "I have to look into this, Chris."

"I know." Barelli picked up her hand, cushioned it in a measuring gesture against his larger hand. "This time I think you may be right."

She looked at him, surprised. The last time she'd tried to figure out a case he was working on, he'd gone into a John Wayne imitation that wouldn't quit. "I thought I'd start out at her house, see if there's anything to get me going."

"We were pretty thorough."

Finny reclaimed her hand but laid it on his leg. "Not thorough enough to find out who did it."

Barelli's eyes narrowed. "Whoever did it, *if* it wasn't Twee, was careful and smart. And lucky, since Twee copped to it."

Finny sighed. "If I'm going skating on thin ice"—she hunched a shoulder at his twisted grin—"and theorizing that Twee's protecting someone with this confession, then the first place I'll look is at Paige Dexter." She met the mocking light in Barelli's eyes. "She *is* Twee's goddaughter."

"And you can't stand her."

"And she's still married to Sarandon. Don't cops usually say that family ties are the ones that kill? I wouldn't want to undermine your confidence."

"Fat chance, I've got male superiority on my side." He

caught both of her hands before they could connect with his ribs. He held her until she gave up trying to tickle him, then brushed a kiss against her lips. He pulled away and looked at her, his eyes unfathomable. "You didn't say anything about the chicken."

Finny frowned, puzzled. "What do you mean?"

"Did you like it?"

"Of course, it was great. Didn't I say that?"

"No, you hardly ate it."

"Chris, it was fine. You know I'm upset about Twee." She ran a hand down his arm.

He got up from the sofa, not looking at her. "Monica always said that the thing she hated most about me as a husband was that I didn't do anything around the house."

"I'm not Monica." Finny stood up. "Now the thing I hate most about you," she murmured provocatively, "is altogether different."

He looked quickly round. "What—"

"You hardly ever throw me over your shoulder and cart me off for wild sex."

"And they say a *woman* works from sun to sun . . ." He scooped her up, ignoring her shriek. "Oof, you've been skipping your exercise class, haven't you?"

"You jerk—"

"Hold still. I mean it—if you don't, I'll end up with a disability pension after all."

"I'll give you disability—"

Seven

"So, I'll come out this afternoon as soon as I can," said Finny. She paused. "Oh. Well, if you're not going to be there . . ." She listened again. "Okay, then, tomorrow. Thanks, Corinne." She set the receiver back onto the phone.

Barelli tossed his comb onto the dresser, his eyes meeting hers in the mirror. "Good-bye construction, hello detection?"

"Yeah. I hate to miss the whole day. But she's got a doctor's appointment this afternoon and said to forget today." Finny turned around. "Hold still." She tugged down the edge of his collar so that his tie was covered. "Power red?"

"Right. Gotta use every advantage for the corporate climb." He cupped her cheek with one hand. "Are you going out to Twee's place first?"

"Mmmm hmmm." Finny tucked her shirttails in and turned to give herself a quick once-over in the mirror. Her camp shirt was pale pink, the pleated pants a dark rose. She'd add the cream-colored jacket when she had to. She could start a whole new fashion trend—the Snoop Look. Did Sam Spade ever worry about color coordination? "I want to look around again," she said. "Try to get a better sense of what happened and when. I just don't think there's any way that Twee could've had time to do in the judge."

"It only took one fast, hard shove. What if nobody's there? The lady of the house being in jail, and all." Barelli tied his shoes.

"Servants, remember?" Finny headed for the bathroom. "There won't be any trouble about my taking a look out there, will there? I assume the police lines are down."

"They ought to be by now. We got a confession." He stood in the bathroom doorway as she applied her makeup. "I can check if you want."

"As long as I don't get somebody on my case for messing with the evidence." Finny waved the mascara wand through her lashes.

Barelli came up close behind her as Revlon brought a hint of blush to her tanned cheeks. "You didn't seem to mind the last time."

"There's no more vacancy on my case, sweetie." She turned around to meet him head on. His shirt was crisp against her cheek and his skin was scented with soap and aftershave. "You smell good."

"Like a rose and that's the way I want to stay."

"Meaning?"

"Roses are for happy, and you're the one who makes me that way. I want you to watch your ass, and if you find anything"—he pulled back a little and looked directly into her eyes—"anything that confirms what you think Twee's doing, you tell me. No heroics. Agreed?"

Her lips curved. "You sound like Miss Kitty."

"Huh?"

"You know: 'Be careful, Matt.' "

"Beats sounding like Chester." He planted a kiss on her lips. "Be careful, Finny."

Traffic on the Valley Highway was thickening like a gourmet's arteries. If the irregular rhythm of the cars was sufficient grounds for diagnosis, cardiac arrest wasn't far off.

Finny slowed down to allow a florist's truck into the stream of traffic off Colorado Boulevard. The Continental behind her honked its disapproval, and she glared into her rearview mirror. Cream 'em, slam 'em, but don't slow down: the Commuter Code.

She fled for her life at the Hampden exit, then wound her way through quiet streets that bordered the Wellshire Golf Course. As she drew closer to Twee's neck of the woods the houses took on stature like a wedding cake takes on frosting, and the lawn verdancy ran the spectrum from chartreuse to emerald.

When she drove through the brick and iron gate that lacked only St. Peter, she felt the usual disbelieving appreciation. Twee's house—make that estate—sat on a gentle hill like a monument-in-the-making, a doily of grass at its base, the Front Range of the Rockies spread out in the distance behind it like a stage set created by the Sierra Club on a speed jag.

Gravel rattled beneath her tires as she pulled around the circle drive and stopped before the portico. Finny once again regretted her lack of a coach and four: a Toyota pickup was so low-rent. As she headed for the entrance, she gave the fender a pat. "Sorry, baby."

The chimes that announced her presence were probably on loan from a European cathedral; the woman answering the door, the maid who'd had so much trouble with trays at the party, was a more local product.

She was a Chicana of about twenty. Her black, wavy hair was barely restrained in a loose knot at the back of her head, her dark velvet eyes were colored with fear, and her mouth threatened to tremble. The blue pastel uniform was pallid against her golden brown skin.

She listened silently as Finny introduced herself, her gaze skittering around Finny as if she were reading unseen information in the air. "What do you want?" She had a heavy accent.

"I don't know if you remember me from the party Sunday night." She waited in vain for a nod. "I'm trying to help Twee—Mrs. Garrett. You know she's confessed to killing Judge Sarandon?"

Now the maid nodded, eyes lowered.

Finny began to feel uncomfortable at the girl's refusal to look directly at her. "I'm trying to find out what happened," she said. "I'm not satisfied that Mrs. Garrett is guilty."

The girl's gaze glanced off her. "You are *policia?*" she whispered.

"No. But I am investigating the judge's murder," she

OBSTACLE COURSE

added quickly as the girl took a step back and started narrowing the open doorway. "What's your name?"

The girl stopped the door's movement. She looked down at the hemp doormat. "Bianca," she finally said in a low voice.

"Bianca who?"

"Lopez."

What was this? Why was she so afraid? Finny took a step closer. "Will you help me, Bianca? Mrs. Garrett has been good to you, hasn't she?"

The downbent head nodded minutely.

"Then won't you let me in, please? I just want to look around, see if anything's been overlooked. Please?" She caught a quick glimpse of anguished dark eyes, and then the slight figure in blue was moving aside. The poor kid was really upset over this, Finny thought. She entered the house quickly, before the girl could change her mind.

"Thanks." Finny looked around the entrance hallway as the maid closed the door. The house was perfumed with its usual scent of furniture oil and sandalwood and held a feeling of comfort, the product of space, cleanliness, and the carefully chosen furnishings.

"What do you do now?" Bianca asked.

"Hmmm? Oh—look around, I guess." Finny walked through the archway that opened on the gargantuan living room. The track lighting over the paintings was off, leaving creativity in shadow. The long table that had groaned under so much food two nights ago was pushed up against the wall. It was empty from end to shining end but for a crystal bowl filled with gilded ivy leaves. Finny wondered if Twee had filled the bowl before she confessed to murder or if such esthetic touches were delegated to the staff while she turned herself in.

The coliseum masquerading as the living room was silent, smaller for the lack of tumult. No string quartet, no people posturing for photographers. Without people, the room was able to display its smaller treasures: glass shelves filled with miniature birds in varying poses; a shadow box filled with ceramic thimbles; in one corner an étagère

53

whose shelves held Russian Easter eggs, ovoid drops of rainbow colors.

Finny looked back at Bianca, who continued to make like a shadow. Did she expect her to scoop up some of the smaller items and secret them in her pockets? "I suppose the police went over what happened Tuesday night, didn't they?"

The maid nodded.

"And they searched everything?"

"Si." She began to move toward the kitchen and Finny followed her.

"Have you thought of anything else since then—anything that might help Mrs. Garrett? I mean, did you see anybody acting suspiciously, or anything that sticks out in your memory?"

"No." Bianca went into the kitchen, crossing the shining blue tiles to the stainless-steel sink. She picked up a rubber caddy filled with cleaning supplies from the Delft tiles of the counter. "I have much work."

Finny came up beside her. The astringent bouquet of household bleach was the woman's only perfume. "Think for a minute. Were you heading back into the kitchen when the woman who found the body ran into you?"

Bianca nodded.

"Before that, when you were getting the tray, did you see anything odd? Or hear anything?"

Bianca seemed to shrink. Her eyes were trained on the gleaming faucet. "Senora Garrett tells me to get the dirty dishes. I get a tray in here and go out there." She gestured toward the living room. "That is all."

"Did you see Judge Sarandon go outside?"

"No. I saw nothing." Her narrow shoulders were stiff.

Finny watched the closed face. "Did you see anyone go outside?"

Bianca looked at the floor. "No."

"Are you sure? Think," Finny urged. "It could help Mrs. Garrett."

Bianca shook her head. Finny could feel the fear that emanated from her.

"I must work now." Bianca's hand reached again for the caddy of cleaning supplies.

Finny spoke slowly. "You seem afraid, Bianca. Is there something I can do to help?"

"No, no. I am not afraid." She spoke feverishly, walking toward the door. "Senor Bartholomew, he says to do my work like always. You must go, please."

Finny followed her. "Would it be all right if I looked around first?"

The girl paused, and the telephone chimed from the kitchen. She nearly ran to catch it.

Saved by the proverbial, thought Finny. What was wrong with the girl? Sure, she'd stumbled across a dead body, which had to be one of life's less glorious experiences, but she acted as though she was facing a firing squad.

"Si, Senor Bartholomew," Finny heard Bianca say. Oh, swell, Mr. Congeniality himself.

". . . a woman called Al-letter," Bianca said, and then her voice dropped into unintelligibility.

After a few minutes, Finny heard the click of plastic on plastic, and Bianca reappeared. She still wasn't looking at Finny.

"Senor Bartholomew, he says you should not be here. He tells me you must leave."

Finny's lips twisted. "I'm not surprised."

For the second time Bianca's gaze met her own. "You will go? You won't make trouble?"

"I may look like a jerk, but I don't always act like one." Finny turned to leave, then stopped. "Here's my card. If you think of anything that might help Mrs. Garrett, will you call me?"

The girl took the card and looked down at it. She nodded.

"Thanks."

"—guess I'm just afraid." The voice was soft and thick with tears. Finny listened in spite of herself, her hand stopped short of the tuning knob. "All my life I've been an outsider. I guess I'm afraid to trust anybody."

"That happens to a lot of people, Angie." The radio

psychologist's voice was warm but brisk. "I would point out that it's only through taking risks that good things happen to people. You might want to consider getting some professional help. If money is a problem, you can get excellent services through your local mental health center. And now I must break; thanks for calling. Thank you for listening to KGBY. We'll be taking more calls after this word from our sponsors."

"Three-minute therapy." Finny muttered. The light ahead turned yellow and she geared down. "Fits into the commercial structure." She turned off the blaring pest control jingle set to the melody of "I Love Paris."

So the maid was a wash. That meant that she'd have to play the old dot-to-dot game: who was connected to whom, and what kind of shape was formed when all of the lines were drawn in?

She turned off University at Quincy and drove east. A stop at a 7-Eleven had resulted in a large Coke and a memory-refreshing look in the phone book. Kit Landauer was at least in it, and he might be willing to give her a phone number for Cuffy Sarandon or Paige Dexter, neither of whom was listed.

As she drove through the land-use patchwork quilt of Cherry Hills, past alternating pasture land and housing developments, Finny rehashed the meeting with Landauer at Twee's party. He'd seemed interested in her until he'd learned that Chris was a cop, which she'd interpreted as snobbery until now. And what about his reaction to Cuffy Sarandon? He's been angry and aggressive, both suspicious in light of subsequent events.

Finny turned into what appeared to be a narrow country lane until she reached its end. The modern wood and stone structure that perched on the gentle hill overlooking a combination of pasture and marshland had as much to do with the deceptive entrance as champagne to potato chips. The bronze XKE parked in front of the house was like a large lion guarding its lair.

The doorbell played the first bar of "Three Coins in the Fountain." The butler who appeared in response came, consequently, as no surprise. "Does Mr. Landauer expect you?" His voice reverberated to full effect, which did surprise Finny, since he was barely an inch taller than she and anorexic in a black suit.

"No, he doesn't expect me. But I'm certain that he'll want to speak with me. It has to do with Judge Sarandon's killing."

The butler nodded. "Very well, madame. I will inquire."

Inquiring minds want to know, Finny thought. She was familiar with the phenomenon.

She couldn't tell by his expression as he returned if the audience had been granted. "Come this way," he said, and measured his steps to the double doors that loomed across the foyer. He pulled them open and stood aside for Finny to enter. "Mr. Landauer will be here presently. You may be seated."

Kit Landauer had had the good sense to decorate his living room around the view framed by the enormous window. The peaks of the Continental Divide, huge, majestic, as removed from the petty concerns of the million-plus humans simmering at their base as the gods whose sentinels they resembled, dozed in the late summer sunshine.

Finny wandered across the silent room wondering, as she often did, how the early pioneers had felt as they inched painfully across the Great Plains in their Conestogas, watching the small hills silhouetted on the horizon continue to grow until they loomed over them like the gates of heaven. Why hadn't they just said "never mind" and spun a one-eighty for the return trip?

The oversized needlepoint brocade sofa called to her, but before she could sit down, she saw the pictures clustered on the dark wooden table. Ovals and squares, most of gold, or could it be platinum? Smiling faces—a shot of a woman on horseback. Finny lifted the frame to look more closely. It was Cuffy Sarandon.

"Finny."

She looked round. Kit Landauer was casual in khaki shorts and a white polo shirt, but his manner was definitely black tie. Tired black tie, at that. The skin around his eyes was puffy and lines bracketed his unsmiling mouth. "Did Hanson offer you anything?" he asked as he crossed the room in a loose-gaited walk.

Ah, Hanson was his name. "No, but I'm fine."

"Well, then, what can I do for you?" He motioned her onto the sofa and waited a half beat for her to seat herself before he took his place at the other end of the tapestried expanse. He settled his tanned legs easily between the sofa and the brass and glass table that held a cloisonné vase filled with pink roses.

"I need to talk to you about what happened Sunday night," Finny said.

Kit shook his head, his golden curls waving like ripe wheat in a breeze. "Why? I've told everything I know—which is nothing—to the police."

Finny cleared her throat. "You seem to have known Twee for a while. I'm hoping you'll have some insight into what might have prompted her to confess to killing Judge Sarandon."

Kit's eyes widened in surprise. "I'd have to say that she confessed because she did it."

"Do you really think she could have?"

Impatience flashed in his face. "I take it you don't?"

"No, and for a number of reasons, the primary one being that I was with her, or saw her during the time she would've had to have killed him."

Landauer raked a hand through his hair. "I just assumed . . ." He laughed shortly. "I can't think of a reason in the world that she'd admit to killing Sarandon if she hadn't done it."

"What if she were covering up for someone? Doesn't that sound more like something Twee would do?"

"What's the point of this, Finny? If the police are satisfied with her story, and you should know, what's your problem? Twee wouldn't be the first person to have a breakdown and kill somebody." His gaze frosted over. "And you aren't exactly privy to the past histories of Twee or the others involved, are you?"

Finny held on to her temper. It must be irritating to be questioned by an outsider. "I'm just covering all the bases . . . and one of those bases seems to me to be that Twee is a generous woman. Just the kind of person to take the rap for somebody she loves."

The animation on Landauer's perfect features would have done credit to a department store mannequin. "I'm not sure what you're implying. Who knows what kind of person Twee is? I've known her since I was a child, but that doesn't mean that I have any idea of what goes through her head on any given day." His eyes met hers coolly. "What fascinates me is that you're so certain about the whole thing. That, and why you'd come to me about it."

Finny raised a brow. "I would've thought you'd be a natural choice." Her lips curled at Kit's look of surprise. "Your relationship with Cuffy. I assumed you were close to the whole family."

Landauer's hand tapped a message on one knee. "I can't imagine where you got that idea."

"How about the way you talked to Cuffy the night of the party? And then there's that photograph of her there on the table."

"I'm afraid you got the wrong impression. Cuffy and I went to Kent together and attended many of the same social functions." Kit stood up smoothly. "You'll have to forgive me. I have a great deal to do today."

Finny was slow in getting to her feet. What was this? "So much that you can't take time to help a friend?"

"Not at all." His gaze didn't meet hers. "I just don't see the point to all of this. I'm as upset as you are about Twee, but I don't think things will be any better because you go poking around in what doesn't concern you."

Finny had been following him out of the room. At his words she stopped. "Wait a minute. It does concern me. What I really came for is Cuffy's phone number. If you wouldn't mind giving it to me, I could—"

Landauer wheeled around and came back toward her. At the look on his face, Finny didn't have any doubts about whether he was capable of violence.

"I think it would be to your advantage to conduct your inquiries elsewhere." His voice was low and civilized. "Twee is an adult and will have to take her own chances with this thing. It has nothing to do with Cuffy or with me. Do you understand?"

Finny didn't relish being close enough to him to count the pores in his chisled nose. She nodded and took a step back. "Good." Landauer turned back to the door and walked through it gracefully. "I really must say good-bye now. I'm very busy." He held the door open for Finny. "I wish you well in your efforts to help Twee. I can't imagine why she would lie about such a thing, but I hope for your sake that she did."

Finny slipped through the door, wincing at the sharp click of the latch as Landauer closed it behind her.

My, my. Mr. Landauer was quite a piece of work, she thought as she threaded her way back to Quincy. For all the urbanity of his words, his face had held nothing but savagery when she'd mentioned Cuffy Sarandon. He'd come on like that at the party, too. Little Boy Blue to the world at large, then gangbusters about Cuffy.

Funny how asking questions had established a whole new sport: throwing Finny Aletter out of the place. That was fine as long as Finny Aletter got something out of it, and so far, she hadn't got nearly enough to justify the exercise.

Finny geared down as she came to a stop sign. She'd always had a fairly low threshold of boredom, and that had definitely been reached. It was time to pick up speed in the old recreational snooping, time to find out what the hell was going on.

TRIP WIRE

HER HAND was tight on the receiver; her other hand trembled as she punched in Miguel's phone number, yet again. With each of the rings a little more of her control dissolved.

"Hello?"

As soon as she heard his voice she felt the hysteria bubble to the surface. "Miguel, she was here, asking questions."

"Who was there? What're you talking about?" The quick, sniffling sound of her breathing told him she was crying. "Slow down, *jita*. Who was it?"

She took in a breath. "The one at the party—*ella se llama Aletter.*"

"What the hell did *she* want?"

Bianca took comfort in the irritation in his voice. If he wasn't afraid, maybe she didn't have to be. "She said she wanted to help Senora Garrett, that she didn't think she'd killed Senor Sarandon."

"Shit."

She listened to the sound of his breath, her eyes focused on the flat blue of the wall.

"What did you tell her?"

"What could I tell her? I know nothing. Senor Bartholomew called while she was here and told me to make her go."

He didn't say anything. Then, "As long as they think Mrs. Garrett did it we're okay. But if this woman finds out something and gets the cops to ask questions, they'll look at you again."

"And then you," she added.

"I told you, I wasn't the one."

"You were so angry."

"*Chica,* I went with you into the house."

"Si. But then—"

"If you love me, you trust me. There's no other way."

Tears filled her eyes. "Si, *te amo.* But you don't tell me everything, Miguel. I can feel it."

His anger filled the silence. "Why do you imagine things to scare yourself? Aren't things bad enough without that?"

"Si." But she waited for him to deny her claim.

"Call me later."

She hung up the phone and leaned her head against the wall.

Eight

FINNY HEADED her pickup onto I-25, toward the spires of buildings that formed downtown Denver. The day was sparkling, a brisk breeze having cleared the air of smog with the thoroughness of a dustrag shaken out a window. The cash register profile of the United Bank Building drew the eye like a bloodstain on a snowbank. It was the only significant architectural variation in a pipe organ skyline of tall glass-and-steel rectangles.

It was nearly eleven when she got to the main branch of the Denver Public Library. However tacky it was to admit it, her collection of books contained neither the *Denver Social Record and Register* nor *Who's Who*. And she'd be willing to bet her left earlobe that Paige Dexter and Cuffy Sarandon were in one or both of them.

She spent the required ten minutes circling the block for a parking space. In the Civic Center, the library was cheek by jowl to the Art Museum, and within spitting distance of the City and County Building, the state Capitol, and the Colorado State History Museum. Not much of that spit ever landed in an available parking place, hence the wild expression in the eyes of locals and tourists alike.

Finny left the library some half hour later, both earlobes intact. Mrs. Paige Dexter Sarandon (née Paige Dabney Dexter), graduate, University of Oklahoma, B.A., member Alpha Chi Omega and at least ten other organizations. She had two telephone numbers listed, one for her residence, one for an office at the headquarters of Dare to Care.

Cuffy was listed under both Paige's and William Sarandon's names, but not to the extent that her address and phone number were included. Apparently she hadn't earned her own listing yet. Finny pondered briefly on what qualifications were entailed, then thumbed through the book for Kit Landauer.

Lamb, Land, there it was, Landauer, Christopher Swain. Born in Denver, partner Landauer & Landauer Interiors, attended Atwood College. Apparently no degree, thought Finny. Member Summit Club, Wellshire Country Club, Boardmember, Rocky Mountain Trendsetters.

Finny jotted down Kit's business number, then leafed through the book for anything else she could find. It wasn't much. Ty Engelman wasn't listed. Les Trethalwyn was. Born in Cardiff, Wales, attended University at Warwick, Graduate of University of Toronto, B.A. director, Denver Arts Consortium. Member, Summit Club. Hmm, he and Kit must be buddies.

A quick check in *Who's Who* added nothing more. Finny slammed the book shut. As reading matter went, it was Boredom City, but it gave her something to work with.

When she came out of the library the carillon bells on the City and County Building were chiming the noon hour. Sunlight was streaming onto Civic Center Park, lighting to a blaze the beds of petunias, their ruffled petticoats of purple and pink fluttering in the light breeze that played across the grounds.

A young Oriental girl was hawking hot dogs and Polish sausage from her pushcart between the park and the library, and Finny succumbed to the scent of sausage and sauerkraut hitchhiking on the midday air. She sauntered past the flowers toward the fountain across Colfax. The chuckling water fell amidst squeals of joy from children clambering over the statue of the horseman.

Finny ate her sausage and contemplated the afternoon's activities. Starting off with Paige Dexter was not her idea of a good time. It was a sure thing that the lady would not welcome her company. Finny detoured toward a garbage can and jettisoned Dixie Cup's answer to Limoges. Like a sign from heaven, the front page of that morning's *Post* lifted on the edge of the breeze. Abigail Hunter, Finny thought. And not more than a block away.

The Denver Post building loomed over her, a pink aggregate and smoky glass spire overlooking both the Sixteenth Street mall at its base and the Front Range in the distance. Other high rises stood at attention nearby, impassively shadowing the traffic canyons below them. Finny crossed at the light.

Heat radiated from the street, releasing a scent of asphalt that combined with the aromas of hot grease and charred meat wafting from a hamburger joint on the corner: the city's summertime perfume. The sidewalks were congested with tourists and late lunchers, armies of legs in motion, the soft thud of men's leather shoes contrapuntal to the serious click-click of women's high heels, the soft soles of sandals and sneakers a gentle, underlying chorus. A high, happy laugh was a short melody drowned by the hissing air brakes of a bus.

Behind double glass doors, the receptionist at the *Post* flashed a professional smile but made Finny wait until she called upstairs to the "Colorado Living" section. "It isn't convenient for Miss Hunter to see you right now," the woman said, one hand over the receiver. Her voice was composed but her eyes blinked nervously. "Do you want to make an appointment?"

Finny's smile was without humor. "Tell Miss Hunter that if I don't see her today, I'll see her in court."

Her message was conveyed with blank efficiency. "Miss Hunter will be right down," she reported.

"Thank you."

Abigail Hunter was not happy to see her. This was evident at the moment the elevator doors swooshed open. Every line of her, stylishly emphasized in a lightweight peach knit suit, was expressive of affront. Each step she took toward Finny captured more territory in the war.

"What do you want?"

Finny studied the aloof face, its even features displayed more prominently by her upswept hairstyle, an intricate French braid.

"Sorry to interrupt your writing," Finny said. "I need a favor."

Abigail's eyes widened. "The hell you say."

"Yeah, the hell I do. If you want to hear about it, I'll buy you a cup of coffee."

She gave the proposition some thought. The glance she slanted at Finny out of the corners of her eyes was laden with curiosity. "Okay. This had better be good."

The coffee shop down the block was nearly empty in the post-lunch hiatus. Abigail was as overdressed for the place as a butterfly for a bog.

"Just two coffees," Finny told the waitress who'd come over to their table on feet that obviously hurt. "Unless you want something—"

Abigail shook her head impatiently. "Coffee's fine." Her eyes assessed Finny's shirt and slacks, finding them lacking. "What's this about? And what was the bit about seeing me in court?"

"That was a bluff." Finny fielded her glare coolly. "I assume you've heard about Twee Garrett."

"Her confession? Nobody's talking about anything else."

"I'm looking into the matter. I don't think she killed William Sarandon."

"Really?" Her long nails, today painted a cinnamon color, drummed on the Formica table. "Do you have any cigarettes?"

"No."

Abigail looked around the room impatiently. "There's a machine. Do you have some change? I came down without my purse."

"Let me check." Finny forked over what she had, and Abigail ventured to the machine, then stopped at the counter to get matches.

"Now, where were we?" She lit up and blew out a long trail of smoke.

"Twee Garrett didn't kill William Sarandon. I'm trying to prove it."

Abigail removed a fleck of tobacco from her tongue with one talon. "Bully for you. What have you got?"

65

"Not much at this point. That's what I wanted to talk to you about."

"Don't look at me. I don't have any vested interest in challenging what the lady says."

Finny's lips thinned. "My interest is in making sure Twee doesn't make a mistake. I'd like to get in touch with Cuffy Sarandon, but I haven't been able to reach her. Do you have her phone number?"

Abigail drew on her cigarette, her hazel eyes narrowed thoughtfully. "What's in it for me?"

"I don't suppose seeing justice done would have any appeal."

"That and—what is it here, fifty cents?—will get me a cup of coffee."

"You want money?"

Abigail's smile didn't extend to her eyes. "Don't be plebeian. I give you the information you want, and in return you agree to let me in on whatever you find out. Specifically, I get exclusive rights to any story that comes out about Twee and her guilt or innocence."

"And you don't care which way it goes, right?"

Abigail ground her cigarette butt in the fluted aluminum ashtray. "High-and-mighty isn't in this year. If you want to play the game, you can come back to the office with me and I'll get what you need."

"Fine. But exclusive rights are going to cost you more. Such as what you know about Kit Landauer and Cuffy Sarandon." Might as well go balls out and damn the expense. "And I want to know the details of what happened between Herbert Garrett and William Sarandon."

Abigail, amazingly, laughed. "You don't want much, do you?"

"Take it or leave it," Finny said. "I'm tired of screwing around."

Abigail tucked the matches into the cellophane wrapper of the cigarette pack. "I may live to regret this," she said in measured tones, "but then again, maybe not. Let's go back to my office."

Finny held the door for her. "Tell me, would you have

acted out of the goodness of your heart if I'd been part of your constituency?"

Abigail's smile would have rivaled a shark's. "My dear, if there's one thing the privileged recognize it's quid pro quo. How do you think they got where they are?"

Two hours later Finny was playing dodge-the-cars in the afternoon rush hour, her mind cluttered with details. Abigail Hunter wasn't one to stint once the deal was made. She'd paid off in spades and added a lagniappe or two to boot.

She'd taken Finny into the "Colorado Living" section of the paper, a large room divided into work areas by the desks and filing cabinets that filled it. Over the sound of ringing phones and clicking computer keys, Abigail had furthered her education.

She referred briefly to a leather-bound notebook and wrote down a telephone number and address for Cuffy Sarandon, then folded the paper in half and flipped it into Finny's lap. "The thing you have to remember about William Sarandon is that hardly anyone could stand him."

"I'd already gotten a piece of that picture," Finny murmured.

"From your tame cop?"

"Well, he's not really that tame."

"Save it unless I can use it in print." Abigail fingered the cigarette pack on her desk. "We can't smoke in here." Her eyes glowed with frustration. "Sarandon was old money—as old as it gets out here. His grandfather started with a gold mine in Cripple Creek, and, instead of blowing what ore he found on fancy ladies and booze like most of his fellows, he invested in other mines. He advanced loans to a lot of the smaller miners, and a hell of a lot of them went broke. They defaulted on the loans and he gained title to quite a few of the claims, which he then mined. By the time the gold and silver rushes were over, Malachi Sarandon had diversified his holdings into cattle and banking, and was rich enough to build up his standing in Denver society."

Finny, perched on the small chair that nestled next to

Abigail's desk like the toadstools that crop up around rocks, nodded, wondering where all this was leading.

Abigail picked up on her impatience. "You'll get the drift. Just hold on." She played with a pencil, her long nails reflecting the overhead lights. "Now, Malachi passed on his fortune to his son, Andrew, who was William Sarandon's father. And Andrew was, to put mildly, a wastrel. By the time he died, he'd run through the lion's share of the old man's fortune and lost another fair portion of it in the Crash."

"Losing his exhalted status in the community?" Finny asked.

Abigail smirked. "It takes more than that. Anyway, William inherited considerably less, in real dollar terms, than his father had. But a part of that inheritance was the claims on the old gold mines. Enter Herbert Garrett."

"Aha."

"Right. William Sarandon was making do with limited interest payments and a small law practice when he convinced his old friend Herbert to form half of Jericho Mountain, the chief assets being what were left of those mining claims and a goodly influx of capital from Herbert."

Finny recrossed her legs for the hundredth time. "They tried to open the old mines near Cripple Creek?"

"The hunt this time was for white gold—a ski resort. At that point it was still possible to get such things done without spending twelve years convincing the EPA that endangered species would thrive under the plan. Herbert was to pay for the improvements, and William signed over pro tem ownership of the mountain as collateral. They would share the income fifty-fifty."

"What happened?"

"A crew was hired to build an access road. The existing survey maps were incomplete, and two men were killed when an old shaft caved in. Their families sued for wrongful death benefits and got awarded a bundle. William faded into the woodwork and Herbert, who had neglected to insist upon a liability clause in the contract with William, got stuck with paying the award as the owner of record. The project was a dead issue after that."

Finny whistled. "But what about Twee and Paige—"

"Twee was still Paige's godmother, and the whole Jericho Mountain deal didn't change her feelings about her. But Herbert didn't want to have anything to do with anyone or anything named Sarandon. Especially since William had gone on to swing a few other deals that feathered his nest nicely, although the birds plucked then weren't quite as prominent. Twee sneaked visits to Paige behind his back until he died."

"What about Paige's and William's separation?"

"What about it?"

"Was it a nasty one? You know, name-calling and divvying up of friends?"

"They were fairly civilized, from what I've heard. I couldn't quote you chapter and verse on the negotiations, although rumor has it that Paige's lawyer got a pretty good maintenance agreement until the final decree. I do know that there never seemed to be much friction when they met at functions, and I guess they weren't in that much of a hurry to split the sheets—they've been separated a pretty long time."

Finny kept silent. Money might be the root of all evil, but it didn't have to be a reason for Paige to kill Sarandon, unless she stood to gain from his will. But surely he'd have changed that as soon as they separated. Then again, who knew what he had done or, for that matter, what the final settlement would have been?

"How do you know all this stuff?" Finny demanded. "You're too young to have been around at the time."

"Too young by a long shot!" Abigail's eyes lit with mischief. "One of the ways people bribe me is to tell me all the old dirt. It doesn't matter where you go, the coinage is the same. There's always somebody willing to tattle for a mention in the column."

"And you just have to hope that the dirt is accurate." Dryly.

Abigail's smile widened. "Denver's big enough so that

I get more than one stool pigeon. All I have to do is compare versions and come up with a reasonable pastiche."

"Swell." Finny straightened on the chair, which was growing harder by the minute. "What about Cuffy and Kit Landauer?"

"That one's not so easy," said Abigail. "I'd picked up enough here and there to know that Judge Sarandon didn't care for Kit. Then, last Halloween, they almost had a fistfight on the dance floor of the Wellshire Country Club. Why, I don't know, but the judge felt strongly enough to put a roadblock in the way of what was shaping up into a sweet little romance."

Finny's gaze held Abigail's hazel eyes. Might as well test the merchandise. "Is Landauer a local product?"

"Oh, yeah. His mother is a Spaulding, as in the floor wax company."

"So Twee isn't the only person with a motive to get Sarandon out of the way."

"Hardly," said Abigail. "Either Kit or Cuffy could have had a vested interest in seeing the old goat dead."

Finny hardly heard her. Landauer had been as forthcoming as a No Parking sign about Cuffy, but why would Twee lie to protect him? On the thought, another idea slid into place. What if Cuffy had killed her father?

Abigail was watching Finny's face with knowing eyes, and when she saw her expression change, she leaned forward. "Remember," she said softly, "whatever you find out comes to me first."

"Will the real Dr. Faust please stand up?"

Abigail nodded. "The devil with a great manicure, that's me. Just don't forget our deal."

Finny got out of the chair. "I won't. One other thing."

Abigail's brows climbed toward her hair. "You're running up quite a tab."

"How about Les Trethalwyn? He and Paige seemed pretty tight at Twee's party."

Abigail shrugged. "I've heard they were once an item, but I think the bottom line is money. He ran through most of his, which is why he's working for the Arts Consortium. Paige has always kept her eye on the bucks. Besides, he's been sniffing around Simms Bainbridge lately. You know, the Bainbridges," she added impatiently at Finny's puzzled expression. "Asphalt."

"Oh, yeah. How could I forget?" Finny pulled her car keys out of her pocket. "Thanks for the information."

Signaling a lane change got Finny the chance to see the lethargic string of cars behind her on Seventeenth metamorphize into demolition derby aspirants, speeding up to block her. A bus lumbered over into her lane as she passed by the Brown Palace. Courtesy of the road. Laying a heavy hand on her horn and veering right produced better results.

So she'd sold her soul to the devil. And for gossip, at that. At least she hadn't challenged the bitch to pistols at dawn. Jigsaws, maybe. That she could handle.

What troubled her most was what Abigail had told her about Cuffy and Kit. If theirs was an nineties version of Romeo and Juliet, then the hunt was going to get messy. She liked Cuffy and wasn't thrilled with the notion of counting the reasons why she might have wanted to kill her father, although she couldn't fault the logic. Killing an obstructive parent made so much more sense than dramatically committing suicide. She'd never had much respect for Romeo and Juliet.

Finny whipped right at Broadway, past the reproduction of *The Thinker* in the window of Columbia Savings. "You and me, kid," she said in passing. He was too intent on his thoughts to answer.

Nine

As Tuesday afternoons went, this was a bust. Finny slammed the pay phone receiver onto its cradle and glared at it. She was hot and tired and her stomach was into replays of its Denver Symphony imitation, despite her sausage sandwich earlier. When the bassoons started winning, it was time to eat. But not in the middle of the fast-food strip along Federal Boulevard.

She'd ended up here after a run to the lumberyard for incidentals—Corinne's cabinet, after all, was still her only paying job. She had to render *something* unto Caesar. The telephone calls from there had netted the same results as the calls made from a gas station an hour and a half before. Cuffy was either going for the world record in conversations or she'd taken the phone off the hook. And Paige was either dancing to the beat of the phone's rhythmic ringing, or passed out in a drunken stupor or had flown off for a quick shopping trip in Aspen. At any rate, she certainly wasn't answering her phone.

Now Finny was starving and there was little relief in sight. McDonald's to the left, Arby's to the right, forward she drove into the valley of the six hundred quick and greasy possibilities: pancakes, tamales, deep-fried fish, et al.; most, if not all, et with a side order of french fries. Pun intended.

The eat-and-run establishments soon gave way to big Victorian houses, which, in turn, led to pre–World War II bungalows proudly displaying their lawns and flowers. The columns of the huge Masonic Temple between Thirty-fifth and Thirty-sixth glowed like browning butter in the afternoon sunshine, and the slow pace of the pedestrians who strolled among the nearby storefronts and cafés befitted the languor seeping into the air.

Finny turned onto Speer and drove toward the heart of the city. The thousands of panes of glass in the skyscrapers, some black, some gold, some the green of an unchlorinated pool, shone, their mirror surfaces reflecting cottony clouds adrift in an impossibly blue sky. Below the viaduct, workers were stringing giant necklaces of train cars on tracks that extended from Denver on either side to both coasts. The Tivoli Center, a wedding cake of a building that had been transformed from a brewery into a shopping center, gleamed, as unexpected among the boxy buildings of the Auraria campus as the Taj Mahal.

That was where she could eat, Finny realized. A bunch of restaurants coexisted there, from Adirondack's to the food court in the shopping area. And she could definitely get a beer. She zipped into the right lane and turned onto Larimer, taking it down to the parking area in front of the Tivoli. She would eat, have that beer, and try phoning Cuffy again. Repletion was just a moment away.

Well, maybe more than a moment. A Reuben sandwich had become one with her flesh, with gusto, and the beer had been drunk, with thanks to Bacchus thrown in. But Cuffy's phone still beeped busy, and her dear mother hadn't answered yet. The inner woman was satisfied, but the nascent detective was pissed.

Barelli always said that police work was tedious. It was finding bits of evidence, trying to make them fit together, and, once in a blue moon, having a kaleidoscopic twist bring everything into focus. Much like her work: cutting, planing, sanding separate pieces of wood until they slipped together like silk on silk, assembled into function and logic. Barelli's efforts usually took place in a milieu of unrelenting seaminess, but she'd so far missed out on that. Her efforts had been among a self-admittedly better class of people.

Of course, she hadn't built much of a case yet—not enough planing and sanding no doubt.

Well, hell, she thought. She also had Cuffy's and Paige's addresses. There was still enough daylight for her to up her social solecism quotient by dropping in for an unannounced visit or two. If she couldn't smooth some wood, she could ruffle some feathers.

The black vinyl seat of her pickup was as hot as the hubs of hell, burning through her slacks enough to make her increase her speed by a good ten mph. She got back onto Speer Boulevard and made for the area's lower rent version of Valhalla: Greenwood Village. According to the address, Cuffy had broadened her horizons by venturing beyond the country club comfort of Cherry Hills Village. Oh, well. Who was she to snipe? If she'd had the money, maybe she'd have wanted the finer things in life: guaranteed tennis courts and the most eclectic collection of Porsches in any neighborhood west of the Mississippi.

University Boulevard would be crammed with commuters this time of day, so she turned south on Downing. By the time she got to Belleview, the roads had coagulated with cars, the BMWs outnumbering the Fords six to one, the Mercedeses coming in first even so. She could rest secure in the knowledge that any dent her little Toyota might sustain would be cheaper to fix than those of the star cars.

Cuffy had a little house at the still-country edge of Greenwood Village, with a half-acre's worth of space for the sleek quarterhorse that watched Finny's entrance on the gravel lane that threaded through wagonwheels planted on either side, like bookends.

The horse trotted over to the wire fence that stretched around the stable built of a two-by-four frame covered with four-by-eight plywood panels. The barnyard element should have clashed with the neat stone-and-brick house that nestled up against the Highline Canal, but it didn't. If the Village had any remaining virtue, it was these pockets of country that had thus far survived the encroachment of expensive architecture and overmanaged landscaping.

As Finny followed the flagstone walk to Cuffy's front door, there was no sign that her presence had been no-

OBSTACLE COURSE

ticed. The mullioned windows were rendered sightless by the wooden shutters visible through the glass, and only the soft nickering of the horse disturbed the quiet.

Finny rang the doorbell. The carriage house lantern over the house number was still on, its yellow light dim and powerless in the bright sunshine. She pushed the doorbell again.

The silence was uncanny. Here, in the middle of a metropolitan area inhabited by over a million souls, the cacophony of freeways and shopping centers was merely a hint on the air. A flicker's insistent tapping on a telephone pole broke the stillness.

"Back to the old drawing board," Finny muttered after a couple of minutes, and she was turning away from the door when it opened.

"Finny?" Cuffy Sarandon had obviously just gotten out of bed. A light cotton wrapper was belted over soft flounces of snowy white cambric. Her ginger hair was mussed and her eyes were bare of makeup. "What are you doing here?"

"Hi, I need to talk to you. May I come in? Just for a little while," she added when Cuffy didn't move.

"Okay." Cuffy stepped back and let Finny into the small living room. It had been decorated in an attempt to replicate a conservatory, with white wicker furniture and pink cabbage roses blooming on the cushions and curtains that were swept back from the white shutters by jaunty bows.

Cuffy glanced out the small stairstep windows in the top third of the door as she closed it. Then she turned, one hand pushing the hair back from her forehead. "What time is it?"

"Nearly four." Finny took a closer look at her. Her eyes were puffy, as if she'd been crying. She looked fine drawn, strained beyond her capacity, her face sharper, older, than the night of the judge's murder. "I'm sorry I woke you. I've been trying to call you all afternoon."

"I took the phone off the hook." Cuffy walked in front of her to the small kitchen, its cheerful yellow walls glowing with the afternoon sunlight. "The doctor gave me some

75

sleeping pills." She turned on a faucet in the sink and held a kettle under the flow, then set it on the stove. "Do you want some coffee? I only have instant."

"Sure, thanks. Uh, could I use your bathroom?"

"Of course." She pointed through the other doorway. "Just down the hall."

Cuffy retrieved the dead phone receiver from the Delft blue countertop and hung it in its accustomed place as Finny went out of the kitchen.

Rosebud wallpaper continued the botanic theme in the small bathroom. As Finny washed her hands, she wrestled briefly with her training: one does not snoop in people's medicine cabinets. One does if one wants to clear a friend of murder, she pointed out to her better self. One snoops like a fiend.

One also finds things. Finny stared at the toiletry items that snuggled next to Cuffy's Secret and Midol. Either she had a more varied life than Finny would have thought, or someone of the masculine persuasion was leaving his Obsession and Mitchum's deodorant behind. Two toothbrushes cohabited cheerfully and an electric razor rested comfortably on the middle shelf.

Finny returned to the kitchen in a pensive mood.

Cuffy had stoneware cups out on the counter and was stirring as she poured hot water into them. She flicked a glance over her shoulder at Finny. "Do you take anything in your coffee?"

"No."

The ensuing silence was thick. One meeting had not a friendship made, especially in light of what had happened.

"Uh, I haven't had the chance to tell you—I'm sorry about your father."

Cuffy, intent upon stirring milk into her coffee, nodded.

"I'm also sorry to bother you now. I wouldn't, except for Twee."

Cuffy stiffened involuntarily. "I'd rather you didn't—"

"I have to. There's something wrong about it, Cuffy. I don't think Twee killed your father."

"Well, that's just dandy." Cuffy turned around. "You do take a lot on yourself, don't you?"

Finny shook her head, unsure of what to say.

"I've never been much on the Miss Manners approach to life," Cuffy said conversationally, "but you really do bring it up. What kind of nerve did it take for you to come here?"

Finny met the anger in Cuffy's eyes. "I'm not indulging myself in a little extracurricular prying. Twee Garrett has been a friend to me, and I don't like the way this whole thing is going down. That may not seem like reason enough to get involved, but it did the trick for me."

"Don't talk to me about Twee." As her voice thickened, Cuffy spoke more quickly. "She's so much more than a friend to me. Do you have any idea how much that adds to the—the horror of all this? Can you even imagine?" She pushed her trembling hands into her pockets. "I think you'd better go."

"No." Finny was beginning to tap into her own anger. "I still can't believe that I'm the only person who can question what's going on. You say Twee's been more than a friend . . . then why the hell are you just accepting what she's doing? You've got a brain—use it! Twee wouldn't kill anything, let alone your father, no matter what he did to her husband. It's been years since all that happened, and yet you and everyone else are just sitting back, saying 'Oh, what a shame. Naughty Twee.' " Finny's voice was getting higher and louder. "Well, that's a bunch of bullshit. And whether or not you lift one finger to try to find out the truth, I won't just let this thing go. Somebody has to help her."

The room was very quiet when she stopped speaking. She had the feeling of fury mixed with embarrassment that often follows impassioned declarations.

"What did you want me to do?" Cuffy asked after a year or two of awkward silence.

"I need information. Who does she care about enough to lie for? Which of those people would want to kill your father? Just the basic, obvious stuff."

"Right." Cuffy again pushed back the hair that fell over

her forehead like a tired paintbrush. "You know who Twee cares about: my mother, me—you, for that matter. She's got a string of foundlings—from struggling artists to the daughter of the man who delivers her booze orders. Would she lie for any of us? I don't know."

Finny watched her sit down at the small kitchen table as if her legs wouldn't hold her up. "Are you okay?"

"Of course," sarcastically, "I feel like a million dollars—which is just a piece of what I'll inherit now that Dad's dead. Does that make me a prime suspect?"

Pulling out the chair across the table from Cuffy, Finny sat down. "I don't want to hurt you, I just want to help Twee."

"And what if you can't do one without the other?"

"I'll jump off that bridge when I get to it."

The telephone rang. Cuffy started at the sound as if it had been a gunshot. She moved awkwardly across the room to pick up the receiver. "Hello? Oh, Mother. Where have you been? I tried to call, but—" She listened, the tears on her cheeks drying, the blurred quality to her features hardening into expressionlessness. "I don't know," she finally said. "Where are you staying?"

Finny watched, wanting to grab the receiver and arrange to see Paige. That would probably be as useful as asking Jerry Falwell to give the convocation at a convention of atheists.

Cuffy's gaze slid over to Finny, who signaled that she wanted to talk to Paige.

"Mother, Finny Aletter is here. You know, Twee's friend from the—from Sunday. She'd like to talk to you." She listened, then, "I'll tell her. I can try, Mother. It's been rather difficult, as you can imagine. Or maybe you can't." Cuffy paused. "I'll do my best. All right!" She hung up the receiver. "Sorry." Her face was tight with control. "Mother's busy right now and can't talk to you. She's trying to clear up some details, like what to do about the funeral."

"I suppose it will be private."

"Very." Cuffy shuddered. "Can you imagine if the

press— Anyway, we won't have a memorial service until next week."

"Do you have any brothers or sisters?"

"No. As Mother always said, once was enough."

Finny felt another spurt of anger. She hadn't liked Paige Dexter one little bit, and nothing she'd heard so far was changing her mind. In the post-I'm-okay-you're-okay era, old Paige had a ways to go.

"The night of Twee's party I saw your mother with a man I used to know," Finny said abruptly. "His name's Ty Engelman. Do you know him?"

Cuffy looked at her. "I've met him. He's sort of drifted in and out of Mother's life for the last year or so. Why?"

"I told you that I wanted to find out about the people who might want to kill your father. There seemed to be, um, some intensity between him and Paige."

"They're sleeping together, if that's what you mean." Cuffy waved toward the phone. "Mother's staying with him right now."

Loyal little thing, Finny thought. Maybe I'm being a tad too diffident in my approach. "Was there any, uh, difficulty in your parents' separation? Do you think your mother would have had a reason to kill your father?"

"Just spit it right out." Cuffy's laugh had an edge of desperation to it. "You have one hell of a lot of gall. You come here, talking about my mother—I'm still trying to deal with the idea of Twee—" she gulped—"killing him."

This wasn't accomplishing much. Finny rose from the chair. "I think maybe we'd better postpone this conversation. Can I call you later?"

Cuffy followed her to the door. "What for? Do you want to take potshots at a few more of my relatives?"

Finny looked into her eyes, bright with tears and malice. So much for friendship. "By the way," she said deliberately, "I saw Kit Landauer this morning."

"What did he say?" The question came as quickly as her swift inhalation.

Interesting. "Not a whole lot. Said he didn't know anything about Twee and didn't feel like speculating. He got downright hostile when I mentioned you."

Cuffy looked down at her fingers, as if she suddenly realized they were clasping each other in a death grip. She disentangled them and looked up at Finny. "I can't imagine why," she said thinly. "And it isn't any of your business anyway."

"That's what you think."

Ten

FINNY WAS DRIVING too fast when she left Cuffy's place. She nicked one of the wagonwheels beside the driveway, gunning the engine as she pulled out onto the street, gravel flying in her wake. Only the fast reflexes of the purple-faced man who veered his Eldorado around her pickup saved them both from an encounter of the closer, nastier kind. That and the right leg Finny used to push the brake nearly into the engine compartment.

"Cool your jets," Finny croaked aloud into the sudden silence of the truck cab. She restarted the stalled engine, then steered her pickup to the side of the road to allow her heart to descend to its usual place.

She turned off the engine and pried the shaking fingers of her left hand off the steering wheel, then pushed her hair off her forehead. The nowhere she was getting fast would be permanent unless she got her frustration under control. It wouldn't do Twee—to say nothing of herself—any good to get smeared all over the pavement.

Okay, so it'd been a bitch of a day. She'd had those before, a lot of them, if she thought back a ways. The only way to deal with hassles was to face them head on. Trying to prove Twee innocent wasn't the same as repairing a staircase or building a piece of furniture. She'd had no part in the creation of all the pieces of this puzzle. Hell, she didn't even know yet what all the pieces were.

A bright red convertible boomed by, its radio turned to maximum audio overkill. The reverberations of "Like a Virgin" punched holes through the quiet neighborhood.

Part of the problem, Finny thought angrily, was the people she was dealing with. There was a barrier between Kit, Cuffy, even Twee, and her. Not to mention Abigail Hunter. Except for Abigail, it was easy to figure out what that barrier was—money, plain and simple. She didn't have to reread her F. Scott Fitzgerald to tune into that. What she'd begun to see up close were the details of the cushion that separated them, the warp and weave of the differences that financial abundance made in the backdrop against which their lives were played out.

She hadn't ever really asked for anything from people of wealth. Until now. It was her seeking help for Twee that had pushed all of the buzz-off buttons among the country club set. Kit Landauer had treated her with disdain. He didn't have to answer her questions and he'd felt perfectly free to threaten her when she'd mentioned Cuffy. She could sympathize. She'd get bent out of shape if somebody threatened Barelli. She loved him, and even though there were some unsettled spots in who they were together, she wouldn't let somebody get away with trying to hurt him.

Okay. What that implied was that Cuffy could be hurt—or that Kit thought she could be. Finny tugged distractedly at the wilting collar of her camp shirt. Cuffy had reacted to her mentioning Kit's name like a duck landing in icy water. She'd definitely sat on whatever she knew, but uncomfortably.

What was uncomfortable were the conclusions she could extrapolate from their behavior. She'd wanted to believe that Twee had confessed to Sarandon's murder to protect some obnoxious soul like Paige Dexter, but if she would sacrifice herself for Paige, she'd be just as likely to do the same for Cuffy. Maybe more so, since Cuffy was infinitely more likable. And Kit's imitation of a stone wall in reaction to her questions about Cuffy could be seen in the same light.

"Shit." Finny couldn't evade the possibility. While she was off getting champagne for the two of them, Cuffy could have followed her father outside and murdered him. Just because it seemed insane to her didn't mean that it couldn't have happened that way. Or, Finny thought, remembering the tension between Kit and Cuffy that night, maybe she and Kit had collaborated on the effort. But would Twee try to protect Kit? If she knew he was involved? It kept coming back to what Twee would or would not do. Murder, no. Balls-out help, maybe. How many people were there in Twee's life who would rate the sacrifice of a confession to murder?

"There's only one way to find out," Finny muttered, and reached forward to turn the key in the ignition. If she couldn't talk to Twee, and the people she *could* talk to wouldn't help her, she would go back to Twee's place and look again. This time she would have something specific to hunt for: photos, names in address books, appointment calendars, lists of birthdays—anything she could find that might identify the people Twee valued.

Finny eased her way back into traffic, her mind on the job ahead. It might not be so easy to get into Twee's house again. After all, MacKenzie Bartholomew had told the maid to give her the heave-ho this morning. But she—what was her name?—Bianca. Yeah, Bianca, had acted so scared that if she couldn't bluff her way in, then she'd forgotten every rotten thing she'd ever learned in the glamorous world of brokering.

Or, Finny thought absently as she downshifted in response to a yellow light, I can take advantage of my newer skills: I could use my wrecking bar to pry open the door.

As the last notes of the stately chimes reverberated behind the massive front door of Twee's house, Finny heard the click of the lock and the knob began to turn. Good thing she'd left the wrecking bar in the pickup.

"May I—you!" Bianca stopped the opening swing of the door with a jerk. She stared up at Finny, eyes wide. Her dark hair was falling in untidy whisps from the loose knot at the back of her neck and she looked both tired and afraid. "What is it you—"

Finny had pushed forward into the gap between the door and its frame. "Sorry to bother you again," she said brusquely. "I need to check out a couple of things I forgot this morning."

"But you cannot." Bianca spread her arms out as if to block Finny's entering any farther, but she was too small and too off-balance to have much effect. *"Madre de Dios,* what are you doing? Mr. Bartholomew, he say—"

"Bianca, what is it?"

At the sound of Twee's voice, Finny's gaze jerked up to the top of the stairs.

Twee, majestic in a long, pink bathrobe, her hair a mass of ragged tufts, stared down in dismay. "Finny!"

She was already halfway up the stairs. "You don't know how happy I am to see you," she was babbling. "All day I've been trying—"

Twee turned in a quick, panicked move and lumbered toward her bedroom door.

"Twee, wait. Please, I have to talk to you." Finny reached the door just as it was swinging shut and she slammed her shoulder against its solid oak surface. "Twee," she said breathlessly, pressing for all she was worth to widen the narrow sliver of space between the latch bolt and the strike plate on the jamb. "Twee, stop it." She could hear Twee's ragged breathing on the other side of the door, and for a moment, she battled an hysterical impulse to laugh.

"Dammit, Twee. Stop it right now!" Finny gained purchase by digging the toes of her running shoes into the sculpted hallway carpeting. She took a half step, then another, pushing steadily with the arms that sawing and hammering had strengthened over the last year.

The matching pressure on the other side of the door suddenly gave way and Finny catapulted into the room, coming up hard against the footboard of the bed, her shins taking the sharp edge of the hard wood.

"Ow!" Finny bent to rub her shins, then cast a quick look over one shoulder to find Twee.

The older woman stood, back against the wall, her eyes closed, a tired, defeated look on her lined face. She had aged ten years since Finny had seen her Sunday night.

Finny straightened as Twee moved, then relaxed as she

came to the side of the bed and sat down heavily. "Twee, I—" she stopped at Twee's upraised hand.

"I'm tired." Twee shook off her pink leather mules and shifted her weight onto the bed. "Why are you here?"

Finny eased round the rosewood footboard, perching on the edge of the mattress as Twee pulled the flowered topsheet and mauve bedspread over her legs. "I've got to talk to you," she said quietly. "You've caused quite a ruckus, you know."

"For whom?" Twee asked coolly. "You? I understand that you've been making something of a nuisance of yourself."

"Now, just a damned minute—"

"Senora Garrett?" Bianca was at the doorway, half in, half out of the room, trepidation on her face. "You are all right?"

Twee's lined features softened for an instant. "Yes, dear. I'm fine. Miss Aletter won't be staying long."

"I—uh, I called Senor Bartholomew." Bianca's gaze lightly glanced off Finny, then skittered past her back to Twee. "He says he is coming."

"Thank you, Bianca." Twee turned to look at Finny. "You probably won't want to stay. I understand MacKenzie threw you out of his office yesterday."

Finny fought the shards of distance that Twee was putting between them. The measured words, and the cold punctiliousness of her manner, had put them, ludicrously, into a familiar, social setting: the Lady of the Manor reproves an importunate acquaintance.

Finny stiffened. "Then he can throw me out of here. I'm not leaving until you've answered some questions."

"I told you I'm tired." With regal disdain, Twee reached for the bedside lamp and switched off the light.

Finny stood up and in two steps was next to the bedside table. She snapped on the light, her forearm knocking over the framed photograph beside the lamp.

Twee lurched upward with an inarticulate cry and snatched up the fallen picture. She cradled it against her chest, dislike radiating from her. "Go away and leave me alone."

"Cut the bullshit," Finny said calmly. "I'm not in the mood to be insulted. I want to know what's going on."

"Not now, Finny." Twee's voice was incongruously frail, coming from such a big woman. "I'm not up to talking now."

"Tough." Finny plumped herself down onto the bed and an invisible cloud of lavender scent engulfed her. She stared stubbornly at Twee. "You've got a lot of explaining to do, and I'm not leaving until you've done it."

Twee looked as forthcoming as a rock, her eyes closed once more, her lips pressed tightly together.

Dammit, Bartholomew would be here in minutes, Finny thought desperately. "Why the confession, Twee?" she said remorselessly. "Who're you trying to protect?"

Twee's eyes opened at that. "I'm not protecting anyone. I killed William Sarandon." Her lips quivered, then firmed. "And I'd do it again."

"You couldn't have. I was with you at about the only time you could've done it." She let out a frustrated sigh. "All right, then, if you insist, tell me the details, Twee. And tell me why." She watched as the older woman lay silent, her breathing jerky, her gaze evading Finny's. What if I'm wrong, her mind pinwheeled. I have been known to be wrong.

"You never knew Herbert, did you?" Twee's lips curved in a soft, sweet smile. "He was the dearest man."

"No, I never met him."

Twee's grip on the photograph tightened. "I met him when I was twenty-nine years old." A coy, flirtatious expression flitted across her strong features. "My mother, my aunts—they'd all given up on me." Her green eyes darkened with memories. "I was taller than most of the men in our set, and as graceful as newborn foal." Her mouth drooped. "One by one, all my friends got engaged, then married."

Finny put her hand over Twee's knuckles, clutching the edge of the bedding. Twee turned toward her, her eyes full of tears. "Herbert was five-foot-seven, and he didn't look like much. He'd just come back from the war, and, except for a small inheritance from an uncle, he was on his own."

She dashed the tears from one cheek. "He had something, though, something I'd never found in anybody else. He believed in himself . . . and he believed in me."

Finny waited for more, but Twee was in the past, her face slack with the memories that moved behind her eyes. "He sounds like a wonderful man," Finny said carefully.

"He was." Twee's voice was dreamy. "Half a head shorter than I, and he hadn't been tutored in the social graces, but he—" Twee's eyes met Finny's. "He made me laugh, and he made me feel small and feminine." One of her hands moved in a vague motion. "He was special, he was a gift. I wanted to give him the world, but I couldn't even have his child." The tears tracked down Twee's cheeks again, and this time she ignored them. "I would have done anything for Herbert." Her face hardened. "Anything."

Finny drew in a breath to speak, but Twee was already going on. "Herbert made money because he trusted his instincts and was wise about the risks he took. But then William Sarandon came up short on capital for his grand new scheme. Skiing would be the industry of the future, he said, and Herbert knew he was right. And William was such a good friend . . ." Her voice trailed off. "When the whole thing failed, Herbert lost his sense of . . . sureness. And without that, he simply couldn't go on."

Finny felt the scratchiness of tears in her own eyes. "So you felt that you owed Sarandon—"

Twee clutched at Finny's hand. "I promised Herbert, when he was dying, I promised him. 'He's a destroyer,' Herbert said, over and over. And I promised him that I would get William. Somehow, someday, I would kill him for Herbert." Twee's anxious gaze lifted to Finny's eyes. "I promised. After everything Herbert did for me, how could I do anything less?"

Finny took a deep breath. "Why so long, Twee?" She produced a smile at the lack of understanding on the older woman's face. "Herbert died years ago. Why did you wait so long?"

Twee looked at her blankly, then finally spoke. "I-I was afraid," she said feebly. "Just scared to do it."

"But you stopped being scared the night of my party?" Finny stared into the clouded green eyes. "After all these years you decided to really kill him?"

"What is going on here?"

Finny spun around. MacKenzie Bartholomew took up most of the doorway, and he was vibrating with anger. "What are you doing here?" he demanded as he strode toward the bed. Despite the hour and the weight of his rage, he was crisp and bandbox fresh down to the knife-sharp crease of his pinstriped trousers. "How dare you force your way into this house?"

Finny pushed herself stiffly off the bed and stood her ground. "I needed to talk to Twee. Forcing my way in was the only way I could manage it."

"I'll see that you're charged with trespassing," Bartholomew raged. "This is a flagrant case of—"

"Stuff it." Finny turned back to Twee. "Get some sleep," she said gently. "You didn't let Herbert down." Before Bartholomew could explode again, she moved toward the door. "We'll talk again, Twee."

She was at the top of the stairs when Bartholomew caught up with her. "I'll have you know that I'm calling the police." His voice was low and deadly. "If I have to, I'll get a restraining order against you. And if you try to contact Twee again in any way, I'll do more than that."

Finny met the ferocity of his gaze blandly. "In your ear, counselor." She walked down the stairs and out the front door.

Eleven

". . . FILED TODAY, seven prisoners in the Adams County Jail bringing suit against the state, citing overcrowded conditions at the facility. Adams County Commissioner Lydell Wolman refused comment. State Senator Miriam Jarvis renewed her drive to subcontract prisons out to private firms. 'Too much of the state's overdrawn resources are being diverted into housing criminals. I appeal to my colleagues in the legislature to look again at the vital role private enterprise can assume in solving this problem.' "

"In other news—"

Finny switched off the radio and dropped her handbag onto the kitchen counter. Her shoulders slumped. She wiped the sweat off her forehead with the back of one hand while the other tugged open the refrigerator door. A six-pack of Coors long necks sat on the first shelf like a treasure waiting for discovery. "There is a God," she muttered. She pulled out one bottle and grabbed the dishtowel hanging from the door handle to twist off the cap. Then the first icy swallow was making its way down her throat.

God, she was tired. She felt as though she'd been run over by a truck. Driven, no doubt, by the outraged scions of the upper crust she'd managed to offend today. Twee would probably be at the wheel.

Finny wandered through the swinging door into the foyer. The mail was scattered under the slot in the door. When she bent to retrieve it, a dust baby shifted slyly at the movement of the air.

She took the clutch of envelopes with her into the living

room, tossing the mail onto the round coffee table, putting the beer beside it, moving on to the bank of shelves and the radio. The message light on the answering machine glowed like a lit cigarette. Finny pushed the playback button.

There were the usual hiccups from people who called but didn't talk. Corinne wanted her to call. Then a musical, modulated voice: "Miss Aletter, it's Les Trethalwyn here. I'd very much appreciate a return call."

Finny jotted down the number given in lilting tones and reached for the phone.

The number was busy. Par for the course. She rewound the message tape and turned on the radio. Billy Joel was throwing his angst around on Mulberry Street as she settled down with the mail, flicking through it like a Las Vegas dealer. Water bill, Public Service bill, junk, junk, a letter from her mother. Wouldn't beat a flush.

Hell, it wouldn't beat a pair. Finny leaned back into the sofa. She hadn't had so many people mad at her since the old days at Lakin & Fulton. But that had just been cutthroat competition. The stuff she was dealing with now had a lot more emotion. She didn't have to be too sensitive to recognize that the hackles she'd raised today among Cuffy, Kit, and MacKenzie Bartholomew were sharp and potentially dangerous. All Bartholomew could do was throw legal jargon at her, but if there was a sliver of a chance that Kit and/or Cuffy had killed William Sarandon, then she probably ought to watch her back.

The irony was that in spite of the waves she'd made, she still didn't know much more than when she'd started. She still thought Twee was lying through her teeth. She might have wanted to kill Sarandon to keep her promise to dear old Herbert, but she'd been about as believable as Richard Nixon when she said she'd done it. And there was still the time element . . .

Congratulations, Finny said to herself. You've reinforced your original theory, but you're as close to figuring out who did kill Sarandon as the Broncos are to a Super Bowl win.

Taking out her frustrations on a blameless haddock fillet

had resulted in a dinner entrée, but no breakthroughs. Her mother had always called fish brain food, so maybe she'd get a moment of revelation after dinner. Sounded like a new liqueur: Moment of Revelation, *for that special time with that special person.* Finny sprinkled more lemon pepper into the cream sauce with a grimace. For that special time when the missing piece to the puzzle is just an agonizing moment away.

Barelli ambled in at about seven-thirty, his jacket draped over one shoulder, his tie loosened and cockeyed. His tumbled hair was damp from the sweat that glistened on his face. "Twee's out and her lawyer has her."

Finny continued pushing the fillets around in their pan. "Yeah, I know. I saw her."

"You're kidding. How'd you manage it?"

"Moral purity." Finny turned off the burner.

Barelli had plopped into a chair, extending his legs and resting his head against the wicker back. "Where'd you get that?"

"Target had a sale." She got out plates and flatware. "Didn't help much."

"So what did she say?" He crossed one ankle over the other. "I take it from the way you're acting that Twee didn't recant her confession."

"On the contrary." Finny tossed napkins onto the table. "She got all choked up telling me how she promised Herbert on his deathbed that she'd kill Sarandon for him. Maybe she thinks she *did* kill him, but I still don't believe her. Dammit, Chris, I feel as though I've stepped into the Twilight Zone."

He was watching her quizzically. "That's an interesting name for it."

"Cute." Finny returned to the stove to dish up the food. "I feel like the guy who invests in bottled oxygen: he knows he's paid a lot of money to buy in but he doesn't have much to show for it. I've got a ton of great motives now, but not one shred of proof."

Barelli's grin was mocking. "So tell me what else you found out."

A half hour later their stomachs were full and Finny

was still beating up on herself. "As far as the others are concerned, I guess I could've camped in Cuffy's living room till she told me about Kit, or I could've bugged Kit some more, but I can't figure out how you lean on people like that."

"Come on, you're talking like you blew it. You didn't. Did you really expect everybody to lay it all out for you as soon as you started asking questions? I'm here to tell you: it ain't that easy."

Finny crumpled her napkin. "I know that. I guess I'm at the point of questioning my basic assumptions. I go off half-cocked, convinced that Twee's innocent, and then I come up against these people who think I'm out to lunch. And to top it off, Twee pulls out the stops to convince me she's a murderer. Shakes me up."

"Welcome to the NFL." Barelli took his plate over to the counter. "Looks to me as if you got several nuggets. One, you're convinced Twee's lying. Two, the atmosphere's definitely thick between Landauer and the Sarandon girl. You just don't have all the information yet. Three, if you got the feeling that something's off-center with the maid, then there has to be a reason. Maybe she has something to hide." The background swoosh of water was cut off at his sharp turn of the faucet handle. "As for Abigail Hunter, I know where to go the next time I have to deal with the high and the mighty."

"You're not exactly her favorite person." Finny wiped the sweat off her forehead, pushing the damp spikes of her bangs back. "I thought I'd hunt down Ty Engelman tomorrow and see what that gets me."

"Engelman. Huh, I don't remember which one he is."

"He was with Paige Dexter the night of the party—or at least that's the impression I got," Finny added slowly. "I was talking to Ty when Paige came up and practically pushed me out of his range."

"You know him?"

"He worked at Templeton Associates about seven years ago. I went out with him a couple of times."

Barelli's eyelids were at half-mast, but he was watching

her with interest. "No kidding. You didn't say anything about it the other night."

"I had other things on my mind." Finny scratched absently around the perimeter of a mosquito bite on her hand. "Cuffy said that he and Paige are sleeping together."

"How cosy."

"I figured it'd be worthwhile to talk to him, if only to get to Paige. But otherwise, I'm not quite sure what to do next."

Barelli shrugged. "Do what we all do: punt."

The ring of the telephone sliced through the quiet, and he picked it up before it could ring again. "Barelli. Oh, hi, Monica."

Finny got up from the table and pushed through the swinging door to the dining room. Good manners were harder to get rid of than cellulite. Somewhere along the line she'd picked up rule number 483: one doesn't listen in on the conversations between one's lover and his ex-wife. One goes into the living room and acts like an unconcerned adult. She caught herself punching the pillows into shape against the back of the sofa and amended the rule: one tries to act like an adult.

She was ripping open her mother's letter when Barelli brought the wineglasses and bottle and set them on the table.

Finny looked at him.

His smile was casual, but his gaze glanced off hers like a ricocheting bullet. "I need to go out for a while, but I thought we could have a drink first."

A peace offering. That meant that Monica needed him to do something for her, and that he was going to do it. "What's up?"

"Oh, one of the fence posts rotted out at the bottom and the dog keeps getting out of the yard."

"Quite an emergency." Finny leaned over to get the wine bottle and fill up her glass. She didn't pour the wine for Barelli.

"What's wrong?"

He had a wary look on his face and that made Finny even madder. She didn't like the way she felt when Monica called, and she didn't like Barelli knowing it and trying to work around her.

"Finny." He was leaning back into the sofa, his dark eyes fixed on her face. "Come on, talk to me."

"What." Irritably.

"Do you remember what we said when I moved in?"

"Love means taking turns cleaning the bathroom?"

"Dammit, Finny." He bit off what he was going to say and took a deep breath. "The stuff about honesty and how that was the only way we were ever going to have anything worth—"

"Okay, okay. I remember."

"So what's the deal? You're upset about Monica's call, right?"

"She calls you every time some little hassle comes up. Why can't her husband take care of that stuff?"

"He's gone again—Washington, I think, and she doesn't have anybody else to call."

Finny blew an exaggerated sigh through her lips. "Why the hell not? I could see it if it was something about the kids—they're your kids, too—but why hasn't she developed other backups, Chris, in two years? Why do *you* keep letting her use you?"

Barelli let his head fall back against the sofa. "She's not like you—she was never independent enough to stand on her own two feet. That was what finally caused the split, because I wasn't around all the times she needed me."

"And you feel guilty."

He didn't answer. He didn't have to.

"I just don't like—screw it." She put down the glass and got up. "I hate sounding like a jealous bitch, Chris. It isn't just that."

"I know." He got to his feet. "I have to go this time, babe."

"Yeah. See you." She walked out of the room. Hell and damn. She was acting like a child. What really bugged her was the hold Monica still had on him. Dammit, she'd dumped him for a lawyer—what kind of *thing* did this woman have for officers of the court?—but she wouldn't take her grasping little claws out of him. Besides, said the jealous little voice inside her, you need him, too. Especially now.

"Finny?"

She turned around and was enveloped in a warm hug. "We'll talk about it when I get back. Okay?"

"Sure."

He gave her a hard kiss. " 'Bye."

She heard the door slam. The hell with it. It wasn't as if she couldn't keep herself entertained. There was a lot more in her life besides Twee's adventures with the criminal justice system. She still had a job to worry about. She'd have time to get caught up on some of her paperwork. Yeah. It was nearly time for the old quarterly income estimate. When all else fails, send off that errant little love letter to the IRS. That and the judicious use of a laxative would make for a regular life, in every sense of the word.

When the telephone rang a few minutes later, Finny was relieved: anything beat the way her thoughts were going, which was straight down the toilet, no puns intended.

"Miss Aletter?" It was Les Trethalwyn.

"Hi, I tried to call you back."

"The phone's been ringing like church bells on Easter Sunday," he said. "It's reached my ears that you're trying to help Twee Garrett in this time of trouble."

Finny smiled at the cadence of his words. "If stumbling around, getting people mad at me constitutes helping, then you've heard right."

"Twee's been very generous with the Consortium. I don't like thinking that someone who supports the arts could be a murderer."

She couldn't tell if he was joking. If her ears were serving her well, a thread of humor underlay the solemnity of what he was saying. She had a sudden image of him, of the twinkle the dark eyes had held when she'd said goodbye to him at the party. He'd seemed interested in her, and this call might be his way of following up on that interest. Nevertheless, he was the only person she'd talked to today who hadn't automatically acquiesced to the idea of Twee's guilt, including Twee herself. It was downright refreshing.

"I suppose a person can kill and still have some esthetic sense," she said. "Isn't that one of the old philosophical arguments?"

"When it comes to philosophy, I'm thinking there's little but arguments."

Finny laughed.

His own warm laughter joined with hers, then died. "I am serious, you know. It's difficult for me to believe that Twee could have stabbed the good judge. It doesn't at all seem her style."

There's a way to view human nature, Finny thought. How one would kill would probably be as distinctive as one's perfume. What a field day Madison Avenue could have with that. "I'm finding that not very many people share your view," she said dryly. "Nobody I've talked to was working too hard to deny Twee's guilt." She didn't think it necessary to tell him she'd talked to Twee.

"Well, perhaps the two of us have more discernment than most, especially considering the competition. It hasn't been that long ago that I heard someone using the rough side of his tongue when talking about the judge."

"Really. Who was it?"

"Now, if I were to tell you that, it might get the person in trouble." His voice was cooling.

"It might also help in figuring out who beside Twee could have killed Sarandon."

Trethalwyn paused. "Ah, you're right. Confession or no, it would take an eight-by-ten photograph of Twee doing the deed to make me believe she would be so crass as to dispatch one of her party guests." The warm thread of humor was back in his voice. "Hell of a hostess, Twee is."

Finny's hand tightened on the receiver. "Yes, she's always been that." A photograph. Damn, why hadn't she remembered before?

"Well, for what it's worth, the person I heard talking about the judge was Ty Engelman. Very adamant he was. I doubt it has anything to do with current circumstances, more's the pity. I won't keep you. I wanted you to know

OBSTACLE COURSE

that I, for one, am appreciative of your efforts, and if there's anything I can do, please call upon me.''

She barely heard him. "Thank you."

"Good night."

"Yes." Finny replaced the receiver. The photographer. As clearly as if he were standing in front of the fireplace she could see his face. Longish black hair brushing the collar of his white shirt. The dark eyes, filled with disdain for the people he photographed. She'd forgotten he even existed. He must have been taking pictures the whole evening. What if he'd snapped something that could help Twee, some shot that could prove she hadn't killed William Sarandon? Or, better yet, a moment that could implicate someone else? But surely the police had talked to him. Chris hadn't said anything about any photographs.

Finny glanced at her watch. Ten till nine. She was at the telephone directory in the next instant, searching through the *H*s, on the lookout for Abigail Hunter's number, more than half convinced she wouldn't find it. And there it was. She snatched up the receiver and rapidly punched in the number. Her personal run of luck held true: it was busy.

And then the rest of what Les had said sunk in. Ty Engelman. The name had been on the breeze today, what with Cuffy's disclosure about him and Paige and now the information Les had given her.

She'd known that Ty was off-center, but murder? Then she remembered the way he'd looked at Paige the night of the party: as if he were parched and she were water.

A chill worked its way down the back of her neck.

TRIP WIRE

SHE WAITED for Miguel to finish in the bathroom. The sound of the shower mocked the hot, heavy air in the bedroom.

Bianca pulled back the blue chenille bedspread from the pillows, then plumped the two pillows into fat cushions. She smoothed invisible wrinkles on the cases, trying to decide whether she should say anything.

He came out of the bathroom on a sigh of steam. Naked, he padded by, resting his hand for an instant on her hip, moving past her to the dresser where he rummaged for shorts and socks.

"Miguel?"

"Yeah?" He stepped into shorts, pulled them up his brown legs.

"What are you doing?"

"Getting dressed." He glanced over his shoulder, his eyes avoiding hers. "Didn't I tell you? Another wedding. I won't be too late."

She played with the top button of her uniform, careful not to look at him.

He chafed at the weight of her silence. "What is it, *jita?*"

She hesitated, then, "What are you doing?"

He looked away. "I told you—"

"No, Miguel. You have been different." She put one hand over her heart. "I feel it here."

He pulled on jeans, zipped them, walked over to her. "Hey, what you doin'?" He held her, letting one hand curve over her belly. "It's the baby—it makes you imagine things."

Bianca closed her eyes. If she could stay right here in his arms forever, everything would be all right. The fear inside her was as alive as the child in her womb. She pulled away from him slowly and looked up into his eyes. "No."

Miguel let his arms drop and he turned away. "You don't need to worry. I'm just working on something."

"What is it?" She watched him as he tugged on his socks impatiently. "Tell me."

"Nothin' important." Sullenly. "Nothin' you need to worry about."

She pressed her hands together. "Miguel, *te amo.*"

"I love you, too."

"Then tell me. You started out to punish him, that judge, for Elena. Now, I don't know. I'm afraid."

He looked over his shoulder at her. His eyes, the deep brown eyes that drew her into his heart, watched her with a coolness that made her muscles tense. "I found a way to make some extra money. That's all, just some extra money for when the baby comes."

She shook her head. "It has to do with the murder, si? Tell me, Miguel!"

His lips twisted. *"Mas vale matar dos pájaros de un tiro."*

"What do you mean?" Her mouth was cotton dry.

"Two birds, *jita*. The stone I'm using will kill two birds."

"Miguel—"

He finished tying his shoes and stood up. "A little justice is all I want, *chica*. A little equality." The sneer was heavy in his voice. "And the only way to get it is to take it. I finally got something to help me."

Twelve

"WHAT PHOTOGRAPHER?" The impatience in Abigail Hunter's voice came over the line as clearly as piped-in music in a K-mart. "I covered Twee's party alone. It wasn't a big enough deal to warrant a photog."

Finny grimaced at her coffee cup. Subtle little thing. "Then who was the guy taking pictures that night? I know he was there not too long before Sarandon was killed."

"I wouldn't know. Maybe a free-lancer. Lots of people hire them and then try to peddle their stuff to us."

"Damn." Finny doodled on the notepad by the phone, cubes and triangles. "I'd forgotten all about him until last night. Where would I find out about him?"

"You're asking me?" Abigail's voice was desert dry. "I'd suggest you ask Twee. She's used publicists before; she may have gone through one this time."

"Publicists?" Her pencil lead moved into the curve of a flying bird—maybe a gull?

"How do you think we find out about all these soirées? Can you see Twee typing up the information about any of her little dos?"

"I see your point. Do you know who she's used in the past?"

"No. Why not ask Twee herself?" Sweetly.

The pencil was shading the blade of a knife. A sharp knife. Gee, if only she'd thought of that yesterday. "Thanks a lot."

"Think nothing of it." The delicacy with which she hung up was in itself a comment.

100

Finny slammed her pencil onto the counter. Sure, she could ask Twee. She'd walk right up to her door and be welcomed with open arms. And a million-dollar check from Publisher's Clearing House would be landing on her doorstep any day now.

Barelli hadn't seen the photographer either. She'd waited impatiently last night for him to get home from playing domestic hero. He was interested in what Les Trethalwyn had said about Ty, but when she'd mentioned the man with the camera, he'd drawn a blank. "I didn't talk to any photographer."

"You had to. I saw him. He looked as though Twee's crowd was the worst thing since receding gumlines. He was near that huge painting—the roadshow Picasso."

Barelli had only shaken his head. "Sorry, babe, didn't see him."

Finny looked at him, her mind racing. "Doesn't that seem odd to you? You ended up talking to everybody at that party."

Barelli ran a hand over his jaw. "I thought we had. But he could have left early, or he might have ducked out before we got everybody rounded up."

"But why would somebody do that if he didn't commit the crime?"

Barelli's expression was cynical. "You'd be amazed at how many people don't like talking to cops."

"Oh, I don't know." She ignored his feint to her chin, her eyes narrowing. "What if he killed William Sarandon? He could have walked straight out the back yard with nobody the wiser."

He raised a brow. "There's a problem with that."

"You said yourself that a lot of people had reason to want Sarandon dead."

"Yeah, but why the hell would Twee lie to cover the photographer's ass? It doesn't make sense."

"Shit." Finny stared sightlessly at a hole in her sock. "Maybe he's a friend of Twee's, the way I am, and she was trying to give him a break and—"

"And to help him out she copped to murder? Come on, Finny. When you start out with a theory, you have to fight like hell to keep from twisting everything to fit it. If Twee's covering up for anybody, she has to have a damned good reason for it. Prison is a long way from the country club. Protecting a photographer is a piss-poor reason to change her residence from one to the other—unless he's her long-lost son, or something.''

"Sure, her long-lost homicidal son. It's all the possible connections among all these people that make me crazy. Dammit, Chris, if I just could have gotten Twee to see sense!"

He put one arm around her shoulders. "Let's go to bed. Maybe she'll change her story."

But day had dawned and she hadn't.

That left Ty Engelman as an avenue for information about Paige. Finny had called him first thing, figuring to beard the lion before she left for Corinne's, only to get a cutsy message tape. Was there anybody who didn't have an answering machine anymore?

"Hi, this is Ty and I'm dying to talk to you. Give me a break and leave your number, hmmmm? I promise I'll call." His purr left Finny feeling as though she should be holding the receiver with a tissue. She left her name in a brusque voice. How the hell did male callers respond to that, Finny wondered as she punched in Corinne's phone number for call-forwarding.

Finny drummed her fingers on the kitchen counter, itching to be at work, hammering, sawing, *doing* something. The morning was ticking right along and all she had to show for it was an elevated frustration level. She searched among the fat volumes of the telephone directories for the memorandum book she'd carried in her broker days.

The gray leather cover was smooth and cool to the touch. She leafed through its pages, glancing quickly over the names—other brokers, contacts, customers. It was as close to a précis of her former life as she could find. Somebody she'd known in the business might be able to give her some leads.

Woody Jordan. He'd be the one to call. He'd worked on Seventeenth Street for nearly thirty years, and what he didn't know about the rest of the inmates flat out didn't count.

His secretary had a low, sultry voice, and Finny recalled the gossip about Woody's emphasis on well-packaged competence. Nobody'd ever known for sure that he slept with the help, but that hadn't prevented strong assumptions to that effect.

There was a short pause after Finny identified herself, then the gravelly roar she remembered so well. "Finny, you sweet young thang. Where the hell you been hidin' yo'self?"

"Jesus, Woody, what've you been doing, taking Texan injections?"

"Hush, now, you know I'm a Suthun gentleman."

Finny grinned. "Southern New Jersey, you fake. "What're you up to now?"

His raspy chuckle tickled her ear and she had a vivid image of him: burly, gray hair tousled, bulbous nose red from sun and drink, baby blues twinkling from fleshy folds. "You wouldn't believe how many people eat this stuff up. Makes 'em figure I'm trustworthy, I guess. A hoot, ain't it?"

"Who do you have to convince you're trustworthy, Woody? The only way you ever lost a client was if he died."

He laughed again. "I'm bored, honey-chile, gotta think of new ways to amuse myself. Speakin' of which, what's this I hear about you swingin' a hammer?"

"Yep, I'm out of the business, Woody. It was starting to get to me. Had to do something to pay the rent and work off the hostilities."

"You gotta job here any time you want it, if you ever get tired of honest work."

Finny chuckled. "Thanks. I'm doing okay with the hammer, but I appreciate the thought."

"Anytime, honey."

"What I called about, Woody, is Ty Engelman. Did you ever know him?"

"Hell, yes. Engelman." She heard a voice in the background and Woody rumbled something about papers. "He's the one that Templeton booted out."

Finny frowned. "What do you mean?"

"Four or five years ago—you were on the Street then, weren't you?"

"Yeah, but I don't remember—"

"Engelman had a thing with one of his clients—a lady who remained nameless, believe it or not. He couldn't keep his pants zipped. Or his head screwed on right. He was never officially charged, but word had it he'd fudged his figures—strictly in the lady's favor, of course."

"You're kidding. I never heard a thing about it."

Woody snorted. "You stopped paying attention to gossip when you got your house and started makin' with the sawdust."

"Yeah, but, my God—"

"Anyway, Engelman got handed his head and was told never to darken Templeton's door again. I haven't heard much about him since then. Tony Spurvey, remember him? Oil shale? Anyway, he mentioned Engelman a year, maybe two ago. Said he was peddling insurance."

"Insurance? You mean like life insurance?"

"Guess so." There were sounds of agitation in the background. "What's the beef, Giselle?"

Finny suppressed a giggle. Giselle?

"Got a couple of clients waiting," Woody grumbled into the phone. "Gotta go."

"Thanks, Woody. I appreciate the help."

"It's gonna cost ya, darlin'." He was putting his accent back on like an extra piece of clothing. "Y'all gonna have to come downtown 'n have a drink with me."

"I'm buying. Don't get too mushmouthed, Woody, you'll trip on your tongue."

"Damn sight better'n tripping on somethin' else, sugah." His deep laugh boomed over the wire. "Y'all take care now."

Finny replaced the receiver, her smile dying as she thought about what Woody had told her. Ty had slipped a fair piece down the ladder professionally. There was always the possibility that the slide had evinced itself in other ways as well. How close was he to Paige Dexter? And what would he be willing to do to stay close to her? So far Ty hadn't deigned to return her call and enlighten her.

The ratchet screwdriver rasped its song as Finny screwed the facing into the cabinet sidepiece. With any luck, the cabinet itself would be ready for finishing by the end of the day. She tightened the screw with an extra twist. She could start the doors tomorrow. Her fingers brushed over the wood in pleasure.

"It looks very nice." Corinne was behind her, a stack of towels in her hands. The sunshine from the hall window sparkled in the lenses of her rimless glasses.

Finny nodded toward the towels. "By next week you'll be able to put those in here."

Corinne nodded. "Old houses never have enough storage space. I think it's because people didn't have as much, even the wealthy ones."

"Mmmmm hmmmm." Finny set the last screw and drove it in. When she glanced around Corinne was gone.

A half hour later, when she went downstairs to get sandpaper from her truck, Corinne was at the sink in the kitchen, rinsing off the strawberries she'd picked that morning. She smiled as Finny went out the back door into the riot of flowers that decorated the backyard.

Fat, old-fashioned roses held sway in the center round bed, a fountain of petals and scent that drugged the bees and slowed time. Bachelor's buttons, nicotiana, four o'clocks with buds twisted tight until the cool of the evening, daisies and snapdragons towering over creeping phlox—Finny moved through the flowery ether, eyes dreamy at the luxury of an old-fashioned garden. Not for the first time it occurred to her that the supposedly repressed Victorians had it all over the sensual excesses of today—the porn shops and X-rated movies and such couldn't hold a candle to the lush opulence of nature.

When she came back into the house, Corinne was holding the telephone receiver. "It's for you."

Finny held it to her ear. "Finny Aletter."

"Hi, Finny, it's Ty. What can I do for you?"

Her fingers tightened. "Uh, Ty, thanks for returning my call. Look, I need to talk to you."

His voice oozed a self-aware smugness that made her teeth grind. "Well, here I am. What do you want to talk about?"

Finny felt a sudden, sharp sadness. He sounded like the kind of sleazeball who considered singles bars his natural habitat. He hadn't been like that when she was seeing him. Screwed up, yes, nauseating, no.

"It's kind of hard to say over the phone." She paused. What to do—lay it out or play verbal footsie? "Uh, I've been trying to help Twee Garrett. You know, about the murder of Judge Sarandon."

"What does that have to do with me?" Ty's voice had gone from syrup to ice cubes.

Finny took a deep breath. "I got the impression that you and Paige Dexter—"

"Wait a minute." The smarmy polish had now disappeared into anger. "What is this all about?"

"Ty, I'm just talking to people who were at Twee's party on Sunday. I don't think she killed Sarandon."

"Finny, I've got business to conduct. Thanks so much for calling." The click of the receiver was loud and final.

"Shit." Finny hung up slowly. Dammit, she hadn't had time to even try to get something out of him.

"—does seem a pity that you're having such problems."

"What?" Finny glanced over at Corinne. "I'm sorry, I wasn't paying attention."

"I'm not surprised." Corinne clicked her tongue sympathetically. "It's like doing *The New York Times* crossword. You get just enough letters to think you're sure to have the word, and then you realize you're not even close."

"That's a fairly succinct description of what I've been doing." Finny rested one hip on the counter. "Except I'm more than a few letters short."

"Well, who can blame you?" Corinne's apple-doll face creased alarmingly with her frown. "When the person you're trying to prove innocent keeps confessing, what can you do?"

Finny smiled at the disgust in her reedy voice. "Well, the one thing I've been trying to do seems to be the last thing I can accomplish: talking to the people close to Twee, especially Paige Dexter."

Corinne let the cool water that trickled from the faucet flow over the berries in her hands. "Have you tried going to her house?"

"Not yet, but that's on the agenda."

"That seems wise." Corinne finished picking over the berries and turned off the water. "What are you going to do now?"

Finny straightened. "Work some more on your cabinet, clean up my tools. Then I'll drop by Paige Dexter's house and see what the lady has to say. I wouldn't be surprised if she knows something about Sarandon's death."

"What, William Sarandon's widow?" Corinne couldn't have looked more scandalized if Finny had suggested that she perform a fan dance on the deal table.

"It's been known to happen."

"Even so." Corinne pursed her lips. "It's unseemly enough that she's entertaining so soon after Judge Sarandon's death, but, if you're right, and she's in any way culpable, then it's outrageous."

Finny frowned. "Did you say entertaining?"

"Oh, my, yes." Corinne waved a thin hand at the newspaper, folded neatly in its usual place on the sideboard. "She's hosting a benefit luncheon today. It's shocking."

"You don't say." Finny glanced at the pendulum clock on the top shelf of the sideboard. It was 10:42. "What time is this luncheon supposed to start?"

"At twelve-thirty. It's being held at the Bellicombe Mansion."

"Ritzy." Finny let the idea rattle around. Paige would have a heart attack if she showed up at the luncheon, which in and of itself was a laudable goal. But the bottom line remained: How the hell was she ever going to find out anything if she couldn't talk to those closest to Twee?

107

"If you left right now, you'd have time to change clothes."

Finny's eyes lifted to Corinne's face. The mischief in the old woman's eyes brought a grin to her lips. "I might have to call you to make bail."

"If you need to, I'll be here." Corinne patted her chest, a little tap-tap with her narrow hand. "Goodness, I can't wait to hear what happens. Promise you'll call me."

"You'll be the first." Finny unbuckled her tool belt and headed for the stairs. "I'll get the tools out of the way before I go."

"Don't be silly." Corinne chevvied her toward the front door. "I'll go up and push everything out of the way. You have work to do. Don't waste any time."

Thirteen

"I'M SORRY, what did you say?" The guardian of the guest list was definitely looking askance, her smile shrinking, oh so slowly, as she peered up at Finny, who was at her most elegant in an off-white linen suit and an "I belong here" expression.

"I was told my ticket would be left for me, presumably with you," Finny said. She'd raised one brow for all it was worth, but it wasn't going very far toward impressing the dragon.

"But I don't see your name here." As she bent her head to scan the list yet again, her lacquered hair reflected the light that beamed down from the overhead fixture, suspended by the large-linked chain that disappeared toward the upper reaches of a ceiling nearly the height of heaven.

"I can only assume that the last week has been just too much for Paige." Finny was trying to decide how one could drawl and sound sympathetic at the same time.

"Oh, of course." Perfect teeth bit at the vermillion lower lip. "Well, it's quite unusual, but I suppose if you just go in, it will be all right. Oh," she added, dimpled fingers catching at Finny's sleeve. "Do tell me how to spell your name for the place card." The fingers of her other hand twitched beside calligraphy pens and heavy bond paper.

"Certainly." Finny spelled her name, checking out of the corners of her eyes for anyone who knew her. She felt as though she were crashing the Mint.

"There, that should take care of it." She waved the

small card to hasten the drying of the ink. "Let me see." She perused the seating chart at her right hand. "I'll put you at table seven—there seem to be some empty chairs there."

"Thank-you." Finny moved on, resisting the impulse to hurry. From what she'd observed, languid and graceful was in, quick and flustered was out. Damn, she hated to play against type.

The Bellicombe Mansion had been built at the turn of the century by Jedediah Bellicombe, who had made his fortune carting goods between St. Louis and Denver. He had erected it to assuage the disappointment of his only daughter's failure to marry into European nobility despite his formidable bankroll and her own passable looks. The architectural expression of his we're-just-as-good-as-you-folks sentiments had resulted in a hodgepodge of German practicality ornamented with such fairy tale touches as a crenellated tower at the angle of the L-shaped structure, with turrets at either end.

Finny had entered through the arched gateway, half thinking that she could make out the spikes of a portcullis in the shadows overhead. As she made her way to the ballroom for the luncheon, she realized that the portcullis was the least of it. Tall, stately stone walls, double lancet windows, and polished stone floors that flowed halfway to forever encapsulated the butterfly colors and Thousand-and-One-Nights scents of the women who filled the air with well-bred laughter and talk.

Finny kept a half smile on her lips as she glided through the shoals of conversation groups, managing disbelieving glances at the tapestries that hung from the faraway ceiling. She returned several nods, at least two from myopic-looking women she'd never met. There was no sign of Paige Dexter.

"I beg your pardon."

She'd run aground. The grande dame she'd bumped into gave new meaning to the color lavender, from the lacquered swirls of her hair to the smart frock that must have been designed for a woman some five sizes smaller.

"No, I beg yours." Finny attempted a real smile. "I was looking for someone."

Her smile was not returned. "Aren't you that Aletter woman?" The dowager's jaw squared with certainty. "You were the guest of honor at the party where William Sarandon was killed." Her eyes, peering from wrinkled flesh, gleamed maliciously. "Twee certainly went overboard on the entertainment that night, didn't she?"

"That's one way of putting it." She decided on her own brand of haughtiness. "And your name was . . ."

The old woman waved away the remark with a pillowy hand. "Twee Garrett would hire Barnum and Bailey to pass the hors d'oeuvres if she thought it would make people take notice of her gatherings." She sniffed. "It didn't surprise me at all to learn that she'd committed her little murder at one of her parties. Besides, she's a Cudlow, you know. Violent people, the Cudlows. And my name is Emeline Hanratty."

Finny's eyes narrowed. "You must be one of her dearest friends."

The old woman gave a refined snort. "We've known each other since our school days."

"Excuse me," Finny murmured, looking over Emeline's shoulder. Paige Dexter had entered from a side door half the size of Rhode Island and was making her way to the head table amidst a group of four or five women who clustered about her like destroyers around a battleship. Her widow's weeds consisted of a lime green dress with cream piping, and had undoubtedly been tailored on her as she stood.

Finny glided through the batches of women who, though still talking, were moving en masse toward the luncheon tables like pilgrims toward a shrine. From the appearance of the head table, its center cunningly wrought into a bower filled with pastel flowers and birds, it was a toss-up as to who was the guest of honor: St. Francis of Assisi or Charles Audubon.

"Ladies . . . ladies, will you please find your seats?" The plea was broadcast through a microphone that spit in accompaniment to the softly spoken words. The thin, tanned blonde standing behind the flower-bedecked podium laughed lightly for the benefit of those who had already assumed their places at the head table. What can you do? her shrug asked.

The thick hum of conversation did not abate. Instead, it moved like clouds of perfume along with the women, who floated like dragonflies—fluttering designer wings—toward the pink lily pad tables. Finny saw Cuffy amidst a cluster of pastel dresses.

Table seven was half full, and as she glanced over her lunch-mates-to-be, Finny realized that she'd been relegated to the farm league. The ambience was that of mended bombazine and *les temps perdu*—the luncheon crowd's version of the back of the bus.

"We have a lot to accomplish this afternoon," said the blonde at the podium, and she proceeded to name the various and sundry people responsible for the day's production.

Finny looked around at the hundred or so women who listened desultorily to the introductions of the worker bees, applauding lightly as one after another rose like prairie dogs from their hills to sniff at their moments of recognition.

"And we must give a great deal of thanks to our hostess, the person who made this effort possible and without whom we would not have come together in such elegance and style. She has persevered through a very difficult time to bring us to this pinnacle today. May I present our president, Paige Dexter."

The room itself seemed to sigh as the women rose to their feet, applauding steadily. Paige made the obligatory resistance to coming to the microphone, then, good sport that she was, graciously proceeded to the podium.

When the tumult had subsided, Paige took hold of both sides of the podium and leaned toward the microphone. Her flawless features were intent. "Christine has already thanked many of the individuals who have worked to assure the success of today's benefit. While each and every one of those people deserve multiple mention, I know we're all hungry and anxious to see what delectables await us." She paused for the ripple of laughter that widened across the room.

Her eyes moving from table to table, person to person, Paige let a note of seriousness creep into her voice. "We have all had the advantage of education. It is vital for women of our position to share our resources with those less fortunate. I'm happy to report to you that this luncheon has generated more than four thousand dollars that will go to the Better America Through Literacy Foundation. I applaud all of you for your involvement in this effort." She began the clapping, her smile growing as her audience emulated her.

She was still smiling when her eyes met Finny's across the tables of applauding women. The warmth in her face faded more quickly than denim in Clorox. Finny held her gaze, taking a certain amount of satisfaction in getting such a reaction. After the last two days, she deserved it.

Paige, unsmiling, removed herself to her chair, as Christine, who had popped back up like a jack-in-the-box, led the recessional applause. "And now," she trilled, "enjoy your lunches, prepared so brilliantly for us by Le Frileux Gourmand."

As she spoke, a tall, dark man, stylish in a gray Italian suit, walked quickly up the side of the dais and slipped into the empty chair next to Paige. As the buzz of recognition spread through the room, Christine shook an admonitory finger at the audience. "This afternoon's speaker has just arrived, and I know from your reaction that we all look forward to hearing what he has to say today. But first let's treat ourselves to this wonderful lunch. Enjoy." She subsided into her chair.

Finny was glancing around for the exits. Former Governor Garrison Hatch, more familiarly known as Governor Grinch, had been on the lecture circuit since leaving office some two years earlier. If he was speaking today in his usual vein, his audience would be suicidal before he finished. In an effort to highlight problems given short shrift in the optimism of the last ten years, Hatch had carved his own niche in the pessimistic underbelly of any given social issue, making it his business to point out the unpalatable facts that tended to get lost in the let's go, let's grow mentality of most public and private leaders. Many of his listeners had gone from admiration of his willingness to tackle the difficult questions to a fierce dread of having to listen to the specifics of his dark vision. Darth Vader had nothing on Governor Grinch when it came to a familiarity with the dark side of The Force.

The conversational rheostat was turned back up, and a smattering of applause broke out as a line of uniformed waiters came through one of the side doors with the first of the plates.

"Doesn't Paige look wonderful?" The conversational gambit was thrown out by the soft, middle-aged woman in gray. Her spaniel eyes were too large for her small face, and her mouth was uncertain. She waited for an answer from the adjacent, mannishly dressed woman whose petulant expression deepened at the remark.

"Considering that Chelsea Roche and her group have done most of the work, I don't see why Paige shouldn't look 'wonderful.' "

Finny was grateful for the arrival of her plate. Whatever the iced oval in shredded gelatin was, it had to beat a discussion of internal politics.

"How lovely, *oeufs en gelee*," crooned the tailored brunette at Finny's right. "How innovative for this time of year, don't you agree?"

"Very creative." Finny tasted a small bite. Spiced, poached eggs in Jell-O, she thought. Whee.

Cunning cuisine came and went, accompanied by conversational forays led by the various members of her table. Having exhausted the clothes, travel plans, and marriage habits of the head table's inhabitants, Finny's table mates had just begun a discreet interrogation of her when Paige Dexter glided up to her side.

"Hello," she said with a smile to the table at large. "I'm so glad you all could come today. Finny." She glanced down at her. "Could I bother you to come with me for a moment?" She flashed another smile at the table. "Will you excuse us?"

Maybe listening to Governor Grinch wouldn't be so bad,

Finny thought as she followed Paige's slim, straight figure toward the door behind the head table. *She's probably got an assassination squad back here, just waiting to get me for crashing the place.*

"All right." Paige whirled round in the shadowy hallway after firmly closing the door. Faint sounds of chaos wafted through with the aromas from the kitchen. "What are you doing here?"

Finny pushed her hands into her jacket pockets. "I've been trying to get in touch with you for two days. This was the best way I could think of."

Paige's pale eyes were cold with anger. "You have some nerve barging in here. I've worked quite hard to get this luncheon put together and I'm not going to let a smarmy upstart like you spoil it."

"Smarmy?" Finny's hands clenched inside her pockets. "Geez, I'm all for ending illiteracy."

Paige's lips tightened into a thin line. "Leave right now. You don't belong here. I won't put up with this kind of intrusion."

Finny didn't move. "Cuffy told you that I wanted to talk to you. Why didn't you call me?"

Paige laughed in disbelief. "Why should I? I don't deal with people like you."

"Not even when they're trying to prove that your godmother didn't kill your husband?"

The short, sharp turning of her head caused Paige's gold hoop earrings to slap against her cheeks. "You don't know what you're talking about. Twee *said* that she killed William. She confessed! Do you have any idea what that's done to me?"

"Oh, yeah. I could tell in there that it's really slowed you down on the old social circuit." Finny looked at the beautiful face, the expensive makeup and clothing. "You've known Twee since you were a child. Do you really think she's capable of murder?"

The nearby statue had more expression in its face than Paige had in hers. "This is a private matter, and not your concern."

Finny shot out a hand to keep Paige from turning away.

115

"It *is* my concern! I think Twee is making some kind of grand, stupid gesture, claiming to be responsible for your husband's death. At this point I don't know whether she wants to protect someone or wishes she'd done it. I would've thought you'd want to find out which. You've got to talk to her."

Paige shook her head. "No. I won't. Twee made her own decision—several of them. I won't see her."

"Won't see who?"

Finny turned abruptly at the voice behind her. Ty Engelman, resplendent in an Armani suit, stared at her in surprise, his thin, poetic face blank.

"Finny? What are you doing here?"

"Trying to get some help for Twee. How about you?"

He ignored her, his gaze seeking out Paige instead. "I thought you might like me to drive you home," he said to her. "You know how tired you were this morning."

Paige's eyes flashed a warning. "I just sounded that way over the phone, Ty. I'm perfectly all right."

"But, darling, you said at breakfast—"

Paige looked back at Finny. "Will you leave now? I've spoken with the police. You have no right to question me."

"Well, actually . . ." Finny forced a smile. "I'd really like to talk to Ty since he's here."

He took a step toward her. "I told you on the phone that I have nothing to say to you."

"Maybe you ought to reconsider," Finny said. "If Twee isn't guilty, you might appear a little suspicious, hanging out with the bereaved widow and all."

Ty sucked in a breath and took another step toward Finny. Paige grabbed his coat sleeve. "I cannot stand any more strain." Her eyes were awash with tears. "You just can't harass us this way."

Ty's hand covered hers. He looked at Finny, his eyes cold. "You heard her," he growled. "Leave her alone." He pulled a handkerchief from his pocket and proferred it to Paige.

Paige took hold of the snowy cloth and used it to dab at her eyes. The elaborate monogram waved under her nose.

LTE. The letters were embroidered in flowing script. Maybe insurance wasn't such a bad gig, Finny thought. What kind of first name would he have to go with Ty? Lickspittle?

"Ty," she said gently. Maybe she could try a little divide and conquer stuff. "How about talking to me while Paige finishes with the lunch crowd?"

He looked down at her with contempt. "I don't have to talk to you. None of this has anything to do with you. Get out of here, and leave Paige alone."

Finny glared at him. "Rumor has it that *you* might have had an interest in seeing Judge Sarandon dead. Like to comment?"

Ty's face smoothed. "You're a crank, Finny. Worse, a half-assed crank, and there isn't a soul who really matters who gives a damn about what you say. Keep away from me and from Paige, or I swear to God, I'll—"

Finny waited for whatever he was going to swear, but he just shot her a look of hatred and put an arm around Paige. They both turned their backs on her and went through the door to the ballroom.

Fourteen

IT WAS the bronze color of the car that caught Finny's eyes. Kit Landauer was camped out in front of the Bellicombe Mansion in his XKE. Cars like that probably came with an automatic parking place.

This little luncheon was rapidly turning into old home week for Twee's former party guests. What a shame she couldn't ask Landauer what he was doing here; Ty Engelman had just demonstrated the unfashionable aspects of the direct approach.

Finny ignored Landauer's shining XKE and sauntered down the cobblestone walk, under the coach pulled by four horses rendered in the wrought-iron arch spanning the fence. A sparrow balanced itself on the coachman's upraised whip.

When she reached the street, she turned right instead of left toward her pickup and walked unhurriedly in the opposite direction, overcoming the almost irresistible urge to look back over her shoulder. As an uninvited guest, she'd forgone the private parking lot, about a quarter acre of gravel that stretched beside the mansion. Lucky for her. She wasn't sure she'd have noticed Kit if she'd driven out.

She kept up her steady pace until she'd gone around the curve that took her out of Kit's line of sight, then took off her high heels and picked up her pace. It was time to advance to the rear. She'd circle around the block and get to her pickup without Mr. Landauer's watching her every move. She'd be the one doing the watching. Ty Engelman might have rained on her parade, but he hadn't flooded it out.

Finny reached the pickup and sneaked a look at Landauer's car as she unlocked the door and slid onto the hot vinyl seat. All she could see was what she thought was the back of his head. At least he wasn't waving at her. She rolled down the windows and settled into her seat. Now all she had to do was wait for something to happen. With any luck she'd end up knowing more than she knew now.

Nearly ninety minutes later, what she'd discovered was that sitting and waiting for someone gave vast new dimensions to the concept of boredom. She didn't have anything to read—neither the owner's manual nor the Denver street guide counted—not that she could read and keep an unwavering eye on Kit Landauer at the same time.

So her eye wavered a little. She'd started by memorizing the cunning pattern of slashes and circles engraved on the red bricks of the Tudoresque hovel to her right, and had proceeded to finishing Corinne's cabinet mentally, from setting every nail and filling the resultant holes, to adding an elaborate inlay in the pattern of stags running across the two doors.

She was hot and thirsty and she had to go to the bathroom. Plus, her panty hose had probably sweated five pounds off each of her legs. She'd also begun to fantasize about what would happen if the police decided to wander through. She'd been sitting there so long, it would come as no surprise if one of the residents called the cops.

Finny was into her fifth version of what she could say to any interested police officer when the castle began to disgorge its inhabitants in clutches of twos and threes. In the afternoon sunlight the women fluttered like pastel leaves in a gentle breeze, grouping here and there for final remarks and quick kisses in the air beside one another's cheeks. Their high, excited voices evoked memories of afternoon field hockey matches in junior high school.

Now the trick was to keep an eye on Kit's car while the party flotsam lapped toward the parking area. Once all the cars started coming out, she'd have a hell of a time keeping him in sight.

After a preliminary starting of engines, the cars came pouring out of the parking area like the animals must have left the ark. With hands fluttering from open windows, the light reflecting off windshields and recent wax jobs, the horns bidding exuberant farewells, the cream of Denver's society, distaff version, sped off into the afternoon.

Landauer's XKE didn't move. Perhaps he was planning on homesteading, Finny thought. God, how much longer was he—

The gleaming bronze door of his car opened and Kit began to extricate himself. Finny glanced at the castle, and saw Cuffy Sarandon making her way down the cobbled walk.

Aha.

Finny was a fascinated audience of one as Kit walked toward Cuffy. When she saw him, she stopped and half turned to go back to the castle. Kit bounded over to her, grabbing hold of one arm. Cuffy stopped and stood stiffly in his hold, her head turned away from him.

Kit talked for a while, then stopped. Cuffy shook her head while she spoke and Kit let go of her arm. Then she turned toward him.

Damn, thought Finny. If only she had one of those long distance mikes.

Kit said something else, then motioned toward his car. Cuffy waved a hand toward the parking area, but she was already walking with Kit. He opened the door for her and waited while she settled herself gracefully into the XKE. When he closed the door, his hands rested for a moment on the handle. Then he went around to the driver's side and got in.

Okay, thought Finny. Here we go. Now was her chance to see if tailing people was as easy as it looked on TV. She waited until she heard the snarl of the XKE, then started her more modest engine. All she could hope was that Kit didn't speed. She'd be left behind in a split second.

But Kit drove his car as though he were transporting nitroglycerin. Considering Cuffy's initial reaction to him, maybe he was simply taking necessary precautions.

Instead of struggling to stay up with Landauer, Finny was hard pressed to remain inconspicuous. Surely the man would notice her pickup if it stayed in his rearview mirror too long, but every time she found a stalking horse to trail behind, it would turn off and back she would be, close behind the inching XKE. Either Kit and Cuffy were having one hell of a conversation, or he'd suffered sudden paralysis in his right foot.

By the time Kit turned into the parking lot of the Moo Goo Fry Pan, Finny felt like swooping out of her pickup and banging his head against his steering wheel a few times. Hey, if it worked for Spenser . . .

Cuffy and Kit had stopped talking, or at least they weren't chatting as they entered the red-trimmed brick building that sported a curlicued pent roof with the restaurant's name in yellow neon script.

As the large red door closed behind them, Finny was faced with a dilemma. Did she wait here, a prospect that had all the appeal of undergoing dental surgery, or did she go in? And if she went in, how could she keep them from seeing her? Hell, she thought as she pried herself out of the truck, if they saw her she could bluff them, buy them a drink and initiate an innocuous conversation. It had to be better than sitting out here.

It would have required X-ray vision for either Cuffy or Kit to observe her entrance to the exotic confines of Moo Goo Fry Pan. The hostess desk was camouflaged by three of the largest dieffenbachias Finny had ever seen. The plants' leaves were almost broad enough to obscure the serpentine dragon that floated, shining and golden, on the black lacquer screen behind the desk. The air was pure sandalwood.

The small, satin figure of the hostess was nearly hidden. "One for lunch?"

"Uh, yes." Finny smiled while she tried to kick her brain into gear. "I'd like a private table, please. And where is the ladies room?"

The hostess was waiting for her as she exited from the maze that had led to the facilities. "Come with me, please." She carried the oversized menu in front of her as if for protection as they proceeded down a shadowy corridor to the dining room. Finny tried to make herself inconspicuous, trailing closely behind her.

She needn't have worried. Passing from the tunnel-like corridor into the dining room recalled stories she'd read in an old issue of *Spelunking Journal* she'd found in her gynecologist's office. As she followed the hostess through a labyrinthine pathway among shrouded tables, she began to wonder if she'd even be able to find Cuffy and Kit. The dim candles at the center of each table were just bright enough to prevent running into the furniture. The ornamental lights spaced far apart on the walls were hardly relevant.

As she sat down at the table chosen by the hostess, she heard Cuffy's unmistakable tones and stiffened, ready to seek cover. As the anger in Cuffy's voice became evident, Finny turned her head slowly to look. She and Kit were three tables away, and very engrossed in each other: negatively, by the sound of the conversation.

"—promised you would let me think about this." Cuffy's voice thickened. "You said you'd give me time. And then you pull this kind of—of harassment."

"Cuffy." Finny could barely recognize Kit's shaken voice. "There's too much at stake here. You can't expect me just to sit back and wonder whether you'll decide to—"

"—and that's the real issue, isn't it?" Cuffy snapped. "You don't trust me enough to let me make my own decisions. You're no different from my father." She laughed, a grating laugh that was nibbling on the edge of hysterics. "Isn't that a piece of irony."

"You want a drink?" The waitress beside Finny's table was dressed in sateen pajamas decorated with machine-embroidered flowers.

Finny barely glanced at her. "White wine, please." She could feel her left ear growing larger as she strained to hear what Cuffy was saying.

"—tell by the expression on your face that you know what I mean."

Finny's lip curled. Either Cuffy had been given a better candle, or she had eyes like an owl.

"I love you, Cuffy. I'm not willing to let you make a mistake about us."

"You're not willing to let me do anything. You want it all your own way." There was a muffled sound as Cuffy surged to her feet, the chair upturned behind her. "I've had more than enough of that, Kit, and I won't let *you* get away with it. I'm leaving."

"No, Cuffy, wait." Kit stood up and went around the table. He grabbed hold of Cuffy's arm.

"Let me go." Cuffy's voice was rising. "I mean it, Kit, get your hands off me, now. Right now—" Her words broke off into a cry of pain.

"Cuffy, for god's sake."

Finny had gotten to her feet and now she went around her own table, her eyes on the two of them. She wasn't going to let him get away with strong-arming a woman.

She bumped into a table, nearly knocking it over. "Cuffy?" The folds of another tablecloth caught at her skirt as she passed by it, and she had to pull it off her to avoid carrying it, candle and all, in her wake.

Finny pushed the candle back into place and glanced up. Cuffy and Kit were staring at her as if she'd just waltzed in from a neighboring crypt. "You'd better not try anything," Finny growled at Kit. "I'll call the cops so fast they'll be booking you before you can ask for your check." She glanced quickly at Cuffy. "Are you all right?"

"What are you doing here?" Cuffy asked as Kit demanded, "Did you follow us?"

Finny raised her hand. "It sounded as though you were in trouble. I didn't want him to hurt you."

"Of all the harebrained—" Kit ran a hand through his hair. "Jesus, I can't believe that you're pulling this—this detective bit. Isn't all this nonsense about Twee enough?"

Finny ignored him. "I have my pickup out front," she told Cuffy. "I'll give you a ride if you want to go."

Cuffy seemed to sag. She bent down and righted her chair, then sat. The dim light created deep shadows over her eyes, masking their expression. "It isn't what it looks like," she said finally. "Kit wouldn't hurt me, at least physically."

"You sounded as though he already had." Finny looked at her over the wavering candle flame. "You didn't want to talk to him when you saw him after the luncheon."

Her face darkened and Finny realized that she was blushing. Cuffy glanced at the man beside her. "It's been a hard time for us lately. We haven't been able to tell anyone and that creates a lot of strain."

"Tell anybody what?"

Cuffy paused and Kit's voice, rough and resentful filled the small silence. "We have every reason to talk to each other. Cuffy's my wife."

The telephone rang the instant Finny walked through the door. Before she could answer, she heard Barelli's baritone from the living room. As she wandered in Barelli was saying, "Hold it, she just came in." He held out the receiver to her. "Abigail Hunter."

Finny grimaced, taking the receiver with all the enthusiasm of a skydiver being dropped out over the Gore Range. "Abigail?"

"What happened this afternoon?" By the sound of her, Abigail was on the prowl.

"What're you talking about?"

"Don't get coy with me. I saw Paige Dexter take you out for a confidential chat at the read-your-way-to-riches luncheon. So what happened?"

Finny dropped her handbag onto the table and plumped down onto the sofa. What a pity the woman hadn't found a niche in government intelligence. She was so well suited for it.

"I was politely removed before I could find out much." Finny could hear the click of a lighter, then the quick inhale-exhale of the first draw on a cigarette.

"Come on, you can't tell me that Paige decided to compare social notes with you. What'd you talk about?"

"Once I realized she wasn't going to clap me into the

dungeons for crashing the party, things got boring fast. She read me the riot act for intruding and that was about it."

Abigail swore fluently. "It's a good thing you aren't trying to make a living doing my job—you'd starve."

"I guess so," Finny said as humbly as she could. She'd be damned before she'd tell this bitch what she'd learned. At least not yet. "I just haven't found out anything worth telling you." Finny caught a movement out of the corner of her eye. Barelli stood in the archway between the living room and dining room. He was gesturing "shame-shame" at her with his two index fingers. She reciprocated with a gesture involving only one finger. He grinned and headed back toward the kitchen.

"Well, just make sure you do—tell me, I mean. I've already delivered on my part of the deal."

"I appreciate that, Abigail." Through gritted teeth. "You already have my promise to do the same."

"Okay. *Ciao.*"

" 'Bye."

"You're going to hell." Barelli sauntered over to the couch, a beer in each hand. He handed her a bottle and sat down beside her.

Finny leaned back into the comfort of the overstuffed cushions. "Who says?"

"The Sisters used to tell me that every time I lied."

"So I'll have company. Besides, if I tell her about what I found out today, she'll splash it all over the paper."

"Really? What'd you get?"

"Cuffy Sarandon and Kit Landauer are married, have been for the last eight months." Finny bent her head so he could get his arm around her shoulders. She kicked off her heels and groaned in satisfaction. "How the hell women are supposed to compete with men and wear those damned instruments of torture is beyond me."

"Remind me to tell you about neckties one of these days," Barelli murmured. "Now give."

Finny yawned. "I gave at the office—or, to be more accurate, at the Bellicombe Mansion and at a Chinese restaurant. From the sublime to the sum dim, that's me."

"Huh?"

She gave him a rapid summary of her day's detecting. "I knew there was something going on between them, but the Romeo and Juliet bit caught me by surprise. Sarandon gave old Capulet a run for his money—the last thing he wanted was for Cuffy to marry Kit, and he let more than a few people in on that information. In addition to the big scene at the country club last Halloween."

"Proving that having money doesn't necessarily mean having manners."

Finny poked his ribs. "Proving that Cuffy—or Kit—had more than enough reason to murder William Sarandon. He's so much in love with Cuffy that he makes the Duke of Windsor look like a lounge lizard."

"So why was Sarandon so upset at his wanting to marry Cuffy? Seems as though they were made for each other."

"Right. In a nutshell, the problem was that Sarandon was a trustee of Atwood College, Gloucester, Mass."

Barelli laughed. "Jeez, you really know how to clarify a situation."

"Patience is a virtue, sweetie." Finny tucked her legs under her. "The only thing I could find out about Kit that didn't fit the usual rich-kid profile was the fact that he never graduated from Atwood. He left in the middle of his senior year."

"So?"

"That year he became friends with a kid from Boston who had made something of a cause célèbre of the fact that he was gay. Guess what student body assumed that because he and Kit hung out together, he was gay, too?"

Chris slanted a look down at her. "You're joking, right?"

"Wish I were. Kit said that no matter what he said or did, suddenly he was hung with the label and it wouldn't go away."

"That's crazy." Chris pulled away from her, sitting on the edge of the sofa. "Just because they were friends?"

"That's a simplification, but an accurate one, according to Kit." At his look of skepticism, Finny got mad. "Come on, Chris. Look in your own backyard. The kiss of death, no pun intended, is for a cop to be labeled as gay. Am I right? Haven't I sat with you at some of the parties and heard some of the comments? It happens everywhere, with the gentler guys, the slighter guys. Academia, athletics, the artistic community—you name it. You get tagged as being gay and the tag sticks. And now that AIDS has people frothing at the mouth, the issue isn't what kind of person you are, or what you've done in your lifetime. It all has to do with tags and acronyms and stereotypes."

Chris raised one hand. "Okay, okay, but what about Kit? What happened to him?"

Finny released a breath. "The assholes at his school would probably have let the thing die down if it hadn't been for William Sarandon. He'd been a trustee at Atwood for five or six years when Kit opted to go there. Kit and Cuffy were already an item, and I'm sure the decision to go to his future father-in-law's alma mater was no accident. When the whole brouhaha about Kit and his friend started up, William heard about it. And being the objective son-of-a-bitch that he was, he immediately flew back to Atwood for a private conference with Kit."

She paused.

"Finny?" Barelli finally said.

She was remembering the two of them, Cuffy and Kit, hands entwined on the table, the look between them as Kit told Finny about Atwood. "I was just thinking how ironic it was. Here was Kit doing a decent thing, standing by his friend, and did he ever get it in the ear. Sarandon was in a prosecuting mode and Kit was shaken enough with the school reaction, let alone the appearance of his sweetheart's father. He ended up making the kind of impassioned speech you'd expect from a twenty-two-year-old and capped it by getting teary-eyed with emotion. That cinched it for Sarandon who hadn't shed a tear since he lost money on the ski resort deal. Being a good constitutionalist, he told Kit never to darken their door again and left. Kit withdrew from school not long after."

Barelli tightened his arm around her shoulders. "And did what?"

"Came back to Denver, started working with his father's company"—her lips spread in a mirthless smile—

"Landauer Interiors, and made the party scene. He and Cuffy were still involved but they kept it sub rosa. It wasn't until the Halloween party last fall that Cuffy was willing to defy her father and act independently. They were married after that little scene. Then Cuffy got cold feet and convinced Kit that they shouldn't tell anyone until she got pregnant. She had it all figured out that that's what it would take to assuage Sarandon's anger. Kit's been trying to get her to go public and hang the consequences."

Chris's eyes met hers. "Is Cuffy Sarandon's heir?"

"Apparently." Finny's smile was tired. "You're getting perilously close to the reason that Cuffy and Kit don't want to publicize their marriage yet. Kit's genuinely adding to the strength of Landauer's Interiors, but the company does need an influx of cash to finance the expansion he has in mind. Cuffy's scared shitless that if what happened comes out, Kit'll be the automatic successor to the title of number one suspect if I'm able to clear Twee."

"God, Finny, you've got to admit that he has one hell of a motive. Or even two or three."

"I know. But he and Cuffy were together when Sarandon was killed. That's what they both say, and I can swear that they were after I left you and Abigail at the bar. Plus, I can't believe that Cuffy would have acquiesced to the murder of her father, whatever the situation."

"Yeah, but I'm not so sure. I've seen people do far worse than that to get back at someone for far less than what Sarandon dumped on Kit Landauer."

Finny nodded. "I know. But, as a certain policeman I know always says, you've got to trust your guts. My guts say that neither Cuffy nor Kit killed William Sarandon."

Barelli's lips twisted. "Of course not, babe. Don't you remember? Twee killed him."

TRIP WIRE

SHE SMOOTHED her hands over her skirt and peered up the stairs. The second floor was shadowed and seemed very far from the bottom of the stairs.

OBSTACLE COURSE

She had a sudden, sharp recollection of the first time Miguel brought her here. He'd taken her picture that day at Curtis Park when she'd gone for the festival. The music had made her cry with homesickness, and he snapped an image of her sadness against the background of motion and color and joy.

The sound of a door opening started her up the stairs. Miguel would be asleep on the tattered green couch outside his darkroom. He would laugh at her for being worried because he hadn't come home. Or he would have left to take more pictures and she would wait again at home until he was finished.

A step creaked under her foot. The rubber edging was worn through on the top step. She went down the shabby hallway to his doorway, the frosted glass aglow with the sun from his eastern windows. MICHAEL GUITERREZ PHOTOGRAPHY.

She knocked tentatively on the door, the noise swallowed by the shadows of the old building. She stopped, and the sound of her timid taps seemed to echo in her head. When the silence filled her mind, she knocked again.

The knob was cold, but it turned and the door swung open. She walked in. The air was heavy and hot and the smell hit her like a scream.

Bianca's gaze flicked around the room rapidly, registering the disemboweled file cabinets, spilled proof sheets and prints littering the floor; the desk, top swept clean, drawers yanked out and upended; the door to the darkroom open, liquid oozing out, darkening the faded linoleum. One stream of liquid was red.

Her legs stiffly guided her toward the darkroom's open doorway, toward something waiting in the shadows. The acrid stench of chemicals mixed with a fetid cloud that threatened to gag her.

He was lying on the floor, half under the table

holding the enlarger, dissected by the shadows cast by the naked bulb overhead. Ribbons of negatives, outsized confetti, lay around him, ends and edges wet from spilled chemicals. The back of his head was a pool of blood and hair, black and red.

"Miguel?" The name dropped into a pool of silence that threatened to engulf her. She should scream. She would if it weren't for the ice. She was encased in ice, from her core to her skin. She could barely breathe, let alone scream.

She took a step, leaned down to touch him, a part of her brain whispering, He might still be alive, the rest knowing he'd been dead for some time. Her fingertips registered the cold, plastic surface of his forehead as her eyes were caught by the drying lines on the dirty linoleum near his cheek. A *B*. An *R*. Her heart nearly stopped. She leaned over him to read what he'd scrawled with his own blood.

BIANCA RUN

Fifteen

FINNY WAS SNUGGLED against Barelli, deep in dreams of doors framed in unsanded moldings, doors leading to huge rooms filled with birds, their wings fluttering in pinks and greens and blues. She was going to sand the moldings as soon as the birds stopped flying around the church sanctuary, and then she'd have the key to the door and she'd—

The shrill summons of the phone chased the birds away, into the ozone, and she was reaching for the receiver.

" 'Lo."

"Let me talk to Chris, Finny." It was Apodaca.

"Chris." Finny nudged his shoulder and held the receiver out to him. "Chris."

"Yeah, yeah." His hand shot out from under the sheet and fastened onto the receiver. "What?" he barked into it.

Finny fell back onto her pillow. A glance at the clock radio told the merciless news: 6:03.

"I thought Trujillo had that covered—" Chris stopped and listened a while. "Jesus, Eddie, how the hell would I—" His free hand was exploring the terrain of his stubbly jaw. "Okay, okay. I'll be there as soon as I can. What's the address? All right." He handed the phone to Finny and let his arm fall across his eyes. "Shit."

"What's happening?"

"Nothing good." Barelli battled his way out of the sheets and sat on the edge of the bed. After a while he reached for the bedside lamp switch. In the sudden small pool of light he looked like a sure loser in the fight to get his engines started.

"I thought you were off today."

"Me, too." He scratched the haystack of his hair. "Something's come up."

"I was hoping that would happen a little later." Finny ran her fingertips down his back.

Barelli turned to grab her hand. "Wanna take a raincheck on that?"

"Mmmm hmmm. If that's all I can get."

"What time is it?"

Finny glanced at the clock. "Six-eleven."

"It's all you can get."

"—twenty-six-year-old Hispanic male was found bludgeoned to death in north Denver early this morning. Police have no suspects in the case. The identity of the victim is being withheld pending notification of next of—"

Finny's hand smashed the snooze alarm lever. After a moment she peered blearily at the light filling the room. The extra half hour of sleep hadn't helped. No more sack time. She had a full agenda today, from sanding cabinets to gathering little bits of information regarding murder. And they say you can't have it all.

She followed the principles of time management as she scarfed down her breakfast. Prioritize—or was it priorize—that was what she needed to do. She'd dealt with Cuffy and Kit yesterday, to her own satisfaction, at least, and, no matter what Chris said, she was keeping them off her active suspects list for the moment. Her little tête-à-tête with Paige hadn't produced much, from either her or from Ty Engelman, although she was beginning to think neither one of them liked her much. She was good about picking up on feelings.

Paige had looked fairly chipper yesterday—especially when she was with Ty Engelman—for someone whose husband had bitten the dust. Then there was what Les had told her about Ty. Maybe checking into Sarandon's will would be illuminating. A visit to the county clerk's office might pay off.

Paige and Ty . . . the two were apparently pair bonding for all they were worth. What Paige saw in him was beyond her; maybe he had acquired hidden talents. She remembered the way Ty had touched Paige: his hand stuck to her arm as if they were both covered with Velcro. Except Paige had seemed pretty nervous about it. Maybe she didn't want anybody to know about Ty. Finny's lips twisted. If that was the case, then she ought to stop looking at him as if he were dessert.

Finny got dressed and dragged herself out to Corinne's. She'd planned to finish the cabinet doors, then start sanding, but Corinne waylaid her as she came through the back door.

"Tell me all about the luncheon," she commanded and handed Finny a cup of coffee.

Forty-five minutes and three cups of coffee later, Corinne was finally satisfied with Finny's descriptions of the decorations, food, and clothes. "And you got to talk to Emeline Hanratty." She shook her head in admiration. "She's been one of Denver's society leaders for over forty years."

Finny looked at Corinne in curiosity. Small, clad in a flowered housedress, her gray coronet pinned tightly to her head, she was the antithesis of the fashionable set. Perhaps following the exploits of Denver's wealthy was on a par with movie fandom. "Emeline?" Finny smiled. "She looked at me as if I were from another planet, one I should've stayed on. She didn't have any kind words for Twee, either."

Corinne clicked her tongue. "She's aged, you know. Perhaps she wasn't feeling well."

"My theory is that she's an old witch." Finny pushed her chair back from the table and stood up. "Oh." She stretched and a yawn overtook her. "I'd better get some work done before lunchtime. At the rate I'm going, your towels won't have a permanent home till the first of next week."

Corinne pursed her lips. "Murder is more important than a linen cabinet. I'm not complaining, am I?"

"Hardly." Finny smiled at her in affection. "I think

you're just as interested in this whole thing as I am, maybe more."

Corinne's hand crept up toward her neck. "Well, maybe so. I don't have quite as much to keep me busy now that I've retired." Her hand patted at her chest. "And you must admit that all this crime is most interesting."

"You'd better believe it," Finny said dryly. "I'll go get started." The phone rang as she went out of the kitchen and she could hear the murmur of Corinne's voice.

Finny was halfway up the stairs when Corinne called to her. "It's for you."

"Oh, hell." She turned around and slipped as the runner shifted under her foot. Damn, she kept forgetting to tack the thing down. She'd probably break her neck before the job was finished.

"Finny Aletter."

"Miss Aletter, I have Mr. Bartholomew on the line."

There was a click and Finny barely had time to wonder—Mr. Bartholomew, what the hell?—when his disapproving voice was on the line.

"Miss Aletter, this is MacKenzie Bartholomew. I'm Mrs. Garrett's lawyer, if you recall."

"Mr. Bartholomew. This is a surprise."

"No doubt." He paused and Finny could feel his discomfort as clearly as if she were in the same room with him. "Twee wants to see you right away."

And he hates it, Finny thought. "All right. I'll get there as soon as I can."

"You don't understand."

Finny waited for him to continue.

"This is difficult." He paused, then cleared his throat. "Well, the long and short of it is that Twee is at Mercy Hospital, and I'm hoping—it would be good of you—" He stopped, then spoke quickly. "She, uh, she attempted to—she tried to commit suicide last night."

Suicide. Twee? Finny drove across town to the hospital in a daze. Twee was one of the strong ones; she always had been. The very idea of her trying to kill herself was impossible to comprehend. Twee spent so much time taking care of other people, it wouldn't occur to her to end her own life. How much did this have to do with William Sarandon's death? My God, what if she really *had* killed him?

MacKenzie Bartholomew was waiting for her in the hospital lobby. He was dressed as immaculately as before, his lightweight gray pinstripe suit and pale blue shirt crisp armor against the kind of informality represented by the blue jeans and t-shirt that Finny was wearing. She almost apologized for her appearance until she caught sight of his troubled eyes.

"She's in a confined area," he blurted out, bypassing the social niceties. "They won't let you in without me."

He turned toward the elevators on the far wall and moved rapidly to press the up button.

Finny followed. "Why did she do it?" She waited for a moment for him to answer and, when he didn't, she got mad. "Don't think that you'll get me into this without telling me anything. I've got to know so that I don't say or do the wrong thing." She grabbed one of his arms and forced him around. "Talk."

He shook his head, upset. "I don't know. She wasn't able to say anything at first. When they'd pumped her—her stomach, all she said was that she was sorry she'd failed."

The elevator arrived, its doors hissing open, disgorging two children and a woman who'd been crying. Bartholomew waited for Finny to precede him through the doors.

"How was it that Twee didn't succeed?"

Bartholomew hesitated. "Her maid called me," he said finally. "She was excited; I could hardly understand her." He turned his head away from the floor lights to glance at Finny. "I decided a visit might be in order. Twee was unconscious in her bedroom. The maid was gone."

The doors slid open and the two of them went down the sterile corridor.

Twee was lying so still that, for a moment, Finny wondered if she hadn't managed to achieve her goal. Then she saw the flutter of a pulse at her temple and knew that she was alive.

Finny stepped toward the bed. Twee's lavender-tinged gray hair was lifeless against the stark white of the pillow. Her skin was gray and engraved with lines of fatigue and the inexorable progress of gravity. "Twee?"

Her head turned on the pillow, and she was looking at Finny. The expression in her eyes brought Finny up short. She read sorrow and defeat, and the contrast between this and the vital woman of the party—even the confused, haughty one of a few days ago—had her fighting tears.

"Gee," Finny said in a gravelly voice, "I turn my back on you and you go and do something stupid."

Twee's dry lips curved a little. "Made sense at the time," she whispered.

Finny reached for the hand that rested on the blanket. "Why, Twee? Why'd you do it?"

She lay, eyes closed, then took a breath and spoke in a thready voice. "The idea of going through a trial lost its appeal." She turned her hand over, and, in a sudden movement, clung tightly to Finny. "You've got to believe that I did kill William."

Finny hesitated, then said truthfully, "Twee, I don't see how you could have."

Her eyes opened and met Finny's gaze. "I know what I did," she said with a little of her old spirit. "I killed William because he cheated my husband and me out of hundreds of thousands of dollars. He deserved to die."

Finny released a long breath. "Twee, remember the night of the party. You and Paige and Les Trethalwyn and I were talking. Do you remember?"

Twee nodded.

"I left to go to the rest room and said I'd meet you later. I ran into William Sarandon and he left to clean off. Twee, I saw you in the room during that time he was away. I heard you at least once. And, when you found me right before Bianca discovered Sarandon's body, you said you'd been talking to former Commissioner Nielsson. Isn't that right?"

Twee nodded.

"Twee, there wasn't time for you to kill Sarandon. I know it and you know it."

Twee's head rolled back and forth on the pillow in negation. "No, that isn't right. I told you, I swore I'd kill William someday. It was the only way to punish him, you see. He didn't care enough about anything except money and position! I couldn't take away his money, and it would have taken too much time and effort to cut away his position. It was my job to kill him. It was my right. Nobody could take that away from me."

Slow tears had spilled onto her cheeks and made their way down her face. "When Herbert died I made a promise. I wanted to do it. I thought about it, tried to decide the best way." Her voice choked into sobs. "I promised. You just keep out of it—I wanted to do it. Understand?" on a rising note. "I wanted to."

"It's all right, Twee." Finny patted her shoulder gently. "Just relax now. It's all right."

Her breathing slowed and the crying subsided. In a few minutes she was asleep. Finny glanced at MacKenzie Bartholomew. He was watching Twee, like a man who was looking at something gone long ago.

She motioned toward the door and he nodded.

"She's asleep," Finny told the nurse who came in as they left.

Finny turned to Bartholomew as they walked down the hall. "I still don't believe her. Do you?"

He had his handkerchief at his nose, was wiping at it with short, quick dabs. "I don't know. If you'd asked me last week if Twee Garrett could commit murder, I'd have laughed. Twee has always been one of the kindest people I've known. Stubborn, opinionated, but kind." He tucked his handkerchief back into his pocket. "She's been so . . . vociferous about it, you see. When she came to me, to tell me about William, she seemed proud that she'd done it. Proud, and fearfully angry when I argued against making a confession."

Finny stabbed at the elevator button. "Dammit, she just couldn't have done it. She simply didn't have time."

The elevator opened its jaws and they entered it. Finny

stared at the floor and Bartholomew reached around her to press the floor button.

"Do you know anything about Twee's maid?" Finny asked.

"Very little. Twee said she'd gotten her name from one of her friends. She seemed to like the girl."

"She seemed so afraid when I talked to her Tuesday. I could have sworn she was either lying or hiding something. Now she's disappeared . . . Do you have her phone number or her address?"

He was patting at his nose once again with his handkerchief. "I suppose we have her job application on file at my office."

"Can you check for me?" The doors slid open and they exited into the lobby. "I want to talk to her about last night."

He studied her face for a moment, his own reflecting warring feelings. "I could do that," he said slowly, deliberating. "You would, of course, have to agree to keep any information I give you confidential."

Finny bit back a retort. What did he think she'd do, take out an ad? And for what, the maid's address and phone number? "I promise I'll be discreet."

He ignored her sarcasm. "Very well."

She followed him to the Tech Center and twenty minutes later she was on her way, the information in hand. The maid, Bianca, lived in Westwood, in one of the poorer parts of the area, judging by the street number.

Finny gunned her pickup into the post-lunch traffic flow on the Valley Highway. Westwood wasn't all that far from the Tech Center, at least geographically, but the distance between the two areas was as vast as differing continents— one well-heeled and homogeneous, the other a melting pot of older Hispanic and white cultures and the new, energetic influx of Asian refugees.

Finny signaled a lane change and veered around an Olds that held sway down the center of the highway. Damn. Twee was nearly unraveled. So upset at the idea that she might've let old Herbert down. Was that it? That she was ashamed she *hadn't* killed Sarandon?

She passed a lackadaisical truck and zipped by the playing fields at Denver U. If she could find Bianca, maybe she could discover what she was so hysterical about last night. And why she'd left Twee alone.

Sixteen

FINNY PULLED UP to the curb in front of the tiny duplex on Irving. The front yard, its tired grass graying for lack of water, wilted behind a fence fashioned from two-by-fours and wire netting. The wood was scabrous with flaking green paint.

She went through the gate, up the crumbling cement steps to a shiny, new aluminum screen door. Finny opened the screen and knocked sharply.

In the hot silence of the afternoon, she could hear children's voices from down the block and the lazy shushing of a sprinkler from across the street. She knocked again.

Damn. Finny let her hand drop and turned her back to the door to look around. At the sound of metal against metal behind her, she turned in time to see the door swing open. "Bianca," she began, then stopped. The woman looking at her through the screen was not Bianca Lopez.

"May I help you?" Her voice was soft, but there was a thread of steel in it that made Finny's antennae quiver, especially when she registered the familiarity of the woman's features. Large brown eyes under straight, thick brows, high, defined cheekbones narrowing down into a square, determined chin. She'd seen that face before.

"I'm looking for Bianca Lopez."

"She isn't here right now." The strain was evident in her voice. "Who are you?"

"My name is Finny Aletter. I, uh, spoke with Bianca a day or two ago. About the Sarandon killing."

The woman took a step backward. "I'll tell her you came by."

"Wait." Finny's hand went to the door handle. She tugged, but it was locked. "If you can help me, would you? It's really important that I talk to her."

"Why?"

"She's the maid for Twee Garrett, and Twee—Mrs. Garrett is in the hospital. Bianca was with her last night, and phoned her lawyer, but she left very suddenly, and I was wondering—"

"You were worried? About Bianca?" She was angry. "Or is Bianca to blame for something?"

"No," Finny said quickly. "You don't understand—I just wanted to talk to—"

"I said I'd tell her." The woman began to close the door.

"Wait. May I talk to you, Miss . . ."

"Parmetter." Her lips spread in a travesty of a smile. "Elena Parmetter." The door closed on her name.

"Wait!" Finny banged on the door. Elena Parmetter! The woman whose court case had caused so much bad feeling against William Sarandon. She hammered again on the aluminum screen door. "Miss Parmetter, please! I must talk with you. Please!"

There was no response. After a few minutes, Finny turned away from the door and went back down the sidewalk to the gate. What had she tripped over here? She'd imagined herself filling in the dot-to-dot picture, discovering an image in the bits and pieces of information she would find. But Elena Parmetter at the house of Bianca Lopez? What dot did you go to after a connection like that? Elena killing Sarandon with Bianca's help? Bianca murdering him on Elena's behalf?

Finny climbed into her pickup and started the engine. This was getting too goddamned messy for her tastes. It was like turning over a rock and watching the bugs scramble for cover. She hated bugs.

The telephone was ringing as Finny came through her front door. What now? was her first thought. It was all she could do to answer it.

YVONNE MONTGOMERY

"Where the hell have you been?" Barelli snarled.

"What's the matter?"

"I've been trying to get you since nine-thirty this morning. I need you to come down here."

And I need a stiff drink and twelve hours of sleep. "I knew my offer this morning would get to you sooner or later."

He exhaled an almost-laugh and the tension went out of both of them. "How would you feel about a quickie at the morgue?"

Finny shivered. "Your location leaves a lot to be desired."

"So does the reason I want you to come down. I need you to look at a body."

The city morgue was located in the basement of Denver General Hospital, an innocuous enough building of blond brick and white metal that perched between Sixth Avenue and Broadway, two of the busiest streets in town. Finny had driven past it a hundred times without thinking much about it. Why did it look so sinister today? Give you three guesses, her mind mocked.

Whee, she thought as she swung into the parking lot. Two hospitals in one day. She owed it all to good intentions and clean living.

Barelli was waiting for her at the main door.

"Eddie was in on the call last night," he said as they walked into the hospital. "They found some photo negatives and when they did a quickie proof sheet, guess what beautiful brunette was on one of them?"

"Moi?" The elevator car was slow in coming.

"And you claim to be modest."

The elevator took fifty percent of forever to get to the basement, but it wasn't slow enough for Finny's taste. "Why would there be a picture of me?" The elevator settled with a thud and its doors slid open. Barelli's large hand enveloped hers as he led the way down the corridor.

"Remember your phantom photographer?"

"Oh, no."

"We'll see."

She was cold. It's just psychological, she told herself. Sure. And knowing that was supposed to make her feel better?

At least she didn't have to watch the white-gowned lab technician pull open a drawer. She'd always decried that in the B-grade movies. Too melodramatic, that sliding out of a body from the coroner's file cabinet, the spooky music rising to a crescendo, the hinted horror that it might move. . . .

It wasn't going to move. The body, draped with a sheet, was already outside the stainless steel bank of drawers. Finny was breathing through her mouth against the chemical odors of the place, odors that were probably psychological, too. Hell, maybe all of this was an elaborate hallucination. She slanted a look downward as the technician pulled back the sheet, exposing a head, its skin gray plastic, its hair sticky-looking black fibers. The automatic defenses were kicking in, their little knee-jerk responses as uniform as goose-stepping Nazis.

He looked so young, his face wiped clean of emotion, the eyelids closed forever on the feelings that had animated his expression. What exactly was it about life that informed flesh? But for that difference he could have been asleep, but that difference was a chasm that couldn't be bridged. What had been a good-looking, vital man was now a chunk of flesh with features that could barely be translated into the face she'd seen at Twee's party. The scrape across one of his cheekbones could have been drawn with purple and magenta markers. Finny said, "He's the one."

"Thanks, John." Barelli cupped her elbow with one hand and urged her out of the room.

"How'd he die?" Finny had to hurry to keep up with Barelli's long strides.

"Somebody bashed his head in." He jabbed the elevator button a couple of times. "I hate this place."

"No kidding."

It was better out in the late afternoon. Finny took a deep

breath, savoring the combined scents of cut grass and car exhausts. Polluted air was a hell of a lot better than no air at all.

"You okay?"

"Sure. *I'm* not dead." She looked up at him. "Who was he?"

"A guy named Mike Guiterrez. He rented out as a freelance photographer—weddings, graduation parties—that kind of thing. Strictly local and small-potatoes local at that, until Twee's party."

"Which was such large potatoes."

Barelli shrugged. "Must've been, for him."

Finny frowned. "Do you know how he came to be working for Twee?"

Barelli shook his head. "So far his story's pretty bland looking, but we don't know a lot about him. We've been through his files—photo negatives, bills, correspondence. Eddie's checking out his personal life. Nothing's been a big number in the evidence department."

Finny pushed her hair off her forehead. "I don't get it. You said there was a picture of me?"

"Yeah." Barelli pulled her over to one edge of the sidewalk. A shift change of personnel had white jackets and surgery-green smocks coming and going, meeting between the hospital and the parking lot like both sides of the Red Sea after Moses had moved on. "Eddie caught it. You were wearing that pink outfit you had on at Twee's party, so I knew it was taken that night. You did say you bought it that day, right?"

"Yeah."

They walked slowly toward the parking lot.

"There were other shots," said Barelli, "And I remembered some of the people we saw that night. You know that blonde with the strapless—"

"I remember."

Barelli grinned at her. "The problem is, there were only eighteen negatives for that roll, the usual is twenty-four or thirty-six."

Finny waited for the roar of a semi heading east on

144

Sixth to die down before she answered. "You think he could've been killed because of the photos?"

Barelli shrugged. "It's worth looking into. You've got Sarandon dead, now the photog dead. There were negatives scattered all around his body and the way his studio was torn up, somebody was looking for something."

Finny leaned against the fender of her pickup. "So what happens now?"

"The usual. We talk to the people in those pictures, we try to find out what Guiterrez was up to. We got a couple of names off return addresses on letters, there was a doctor's bill . . . we'll follow up on those. We'll talk to Twee, find out what she knows about him. It all comes down to hustling for whatever information we can get."

Finny closed her eyes, lifting her face to the sun. "Yeah."

Barelli's hand cupped her cheek. "You look tired, babe. Hard day?"

Finny opened her eyes. "Busy, anyway. Twee's lawyer called me this morning at Corinne's."

Barelli arched one brow. "Did he have a religious conversion, or what? Wasn't it a couple of days ago that he threw you out of Twee's house?"

"Having his client attempt suicide seemed to have had quite an impact on his attitude." Finny shook her head. "He passed on her request that I come see her."

Barelli was staring down at her. "His client? You mean Twee tried to kill herself?"

"Didn't you know?" Finny looked up at him, nonplussed. "I thought the police were told about suicides—or the attempts, for that matter."

"Not necessarily. What happened?"

Suddenly he was all cop, and Finny could feel the conversational mode switch into serious business. "She swallowed half a bottle of barbiturates, with pure Smirnoff as a chaser. If it hadn't been for her maid, she would've cashed in her chips for sure."

"Jesus."

She told him about the visit to Twee because of her theory that Bianca Lopez's nonappearance might shed

145

some light on something. "But here's the biggie, Chris. When I went out to her house, she wasn't there. But somebody else was. You'll never guess who."

"The ghost of William Sarandon, right?"

Finny snorted. "Little do you realize. Elena Parmetter answered the door, told me Bianca wasn't there. Now go figure that one out."

"Elena Parmetter." He was looking at her, but Finny had the feeling that he didn't even see her. "What time did Twee check into the hospital, do you know?" His voice was grim.

"No, but I can check. Why?"

"Why?" Barelli ran a hand through his hair. "Finny, the woman confessed to killing William Sarandon. Now the photographer who was at the party that night turns up dead. Her maid is missing and Elena Parmetter, who was the victim of blatant defendant-bashing by William Sarandon, shows up at the maid's house. This is beginning to look like something out of the conspiracy handbook. We've got to check out any connections between Sarandon's and Guiterrez's murders."

"Just don't focus on Twee," Finny said. "Bianca was there the night of the party. She splits the scene last night and Twee tries suicide." Finny looked up into Barelli's eyes. "Mike Guiterrez turns up dead. What if *she's* your killer, Chris. What if Bianca Lopez is behind all of this?"

"Finny." Barelli jammed his hands into his pockets. Probably to prevent himself from strangling her, judging by the frustrated expression on his face. "What screws up everything is Twee's confession. I can't see her as a compulsive confessor. We get them, you know. I had a guy a couple of years ago who admitted to slicing up his wife and planting the pieces under the trees at City Park. He had me going, ready to start looking for a shovel. Came to find out his wife had died the month before of cancer and he was all fucked up with guilt because he hadn't believed she was that sick."

He dug a piece of gum out of one pocket and unwrapped it. "Twee Garrett isn't one of those people who feel so guilty over something they have or haven't done in their lives that they'll read about a crime and then confess to it, wanting to be punished."

"I think you're dead wrong," Finny said. "You should've heard her today. She was practically hysterical, going on and on about how she promised Herbert she'd get even with Sarandon for the way he cheated them. I swear, Chris, it was the old death-bed promise and blood-feud revenge twisted together. The more I said she couldn't have done it, the wilder she got in telling me how she did." Finny pushed her bangs off her forehead. "I think she wanted to kill him, wanted to bad, but she didn't, and now she's working like hell to convince herself she did."

"That's crazy."

Finny frowned. "I didn't say she was sane, Chris. I'm just saying that she's not a killer. Maybe Bianca Lopez is."

One murderer in the hand was worth two in theory, or so Barelli seemed to think. He and Finny had continued their discussion long enough to make for an impressive headache, at least on her part. After his phone call to headquarters they'd found bad coffee and limp sandwiches at a mom-and-pop diner on south Broadway. Finny picked over the meal, her appetite absent despite having missed lunch.

Her protestations about Twee's motives hadn't moved Barelli. "If you start out trying to find a motive, you're working from the wrong end of the thing. You need opportunity and means. If you're lucky, the motive will fall into line behind the two."

"But she wasn't anywhere near Zuni and Thirty-eighth last night."

Barelli looked at her impatiently. "How do you *know* that?"

"You just told me you'd checked with her driver as a 'part of the routine investigation,' and that he hadn't taken her there," Finny snapped. "How the hell—"

"Presumably the lady can drive, she could've called a cab—there are ways, you know." Barelli made a tent of his hands and leaned toward her, sitting across the table from him. "Look, Finny. I can't afford to let my liking for Twee, or my relationship with you, for that matter, affect my thinking about this. Twee was out of jail, Twee's still claiming to have killed Sarandon, Twee tried to kill herself last night—and that, by the way, would probably convict her in just about any jury's eyes. What better reason can you have to kill yourself than remorse for killing someone else?"

"How about trying to clear a friend of murder? Seems like a hell of a reason to me." Finny rubbed at her temples with her fingers. "Dammit, Chris, you said yourself that you thought whoever killed Guiterrez wanted negatives and pictures that were at his studio. That's *got* to eliminate Twee. Why the hell would she worry about incriminating photographs—she's already confessed to killing Sarandon. Who knows what's going on with this Bianca Lopez? Especially now that the connection with Elena Parmetter's come up?"

"Speaking of which," Barelli slid out of the booth and dug in his pocket for change. "Eddie ought to be back by now. Maybe he's found out something about Parmetter and Lopez."

Finny was digging through her handbag for aspirin when he came back to the table. "Did he get anything?" Her voice trailed off as she got a good look at his face. "What is it?"

Barelli folded his long legs under the table and met her concerned gaze squarely. "You aren't going to like it, babe. Mike Guiterrez was Elena Parmetter's cousin. He and Bianca Lopez have been living together for the last six months or so. Elena went over to tell Bianca after Guiterrez's parents were notified about his death. Bianca never came home."

"Maybe she didn't need to be told."

Chris frowned. "It won't wash, Finny. According to Elena, Bianca Lopez is pregnant with Guiterrez's baby."

Finny's eyes widened. "So where the hell *is* she?"

"I wish to God I knew. Eddie said Elena's frantic, trying to figure out where she'd hide."

"Dammit," Finny exploded, "Why—"

"She's an illegal alien," Barelli said. "She's scared to death that if the authorities get hold of her, she'll be deported."

TRIP WIRE ─────────────────────────────────

SHE HAD TO go back for the money. It wasn't much but it was all she had.

The shadows from the old elms across the street were lengthening in the dusk, lapping over the sagging fence when she went through the gate. She looked behind her, then to each side before she pushed the key into the lock. The knob twisted under her hand and she shoved against the warped door to force it open. She slid through the opening, her eyes searching the room, looking for changes, for evidence of someone's presence.

Bianca saw the paper pinned on the sofa back almost immediately. Her heart gave a jump and she stopped, holding her breath, striving to hear any careless sounds from the other rooms.

The silence was a threatening thing, almost worse than the unknown that waited. She ran trembling hands down her thighs, pressing the limp skirt against them. Miguel, she thought, Miguel.

She took a step toward the sofa and the crackle of paper under her foot filled the quiet room. Bending down, she picked up the day's mail where it had fallen from the slot in the door.

Without interest she glanced through the envelopes, the photography magazine. What difference did these make to her? His letter was on the bottom, the neat, slanted writing spelling out her own name in black ink.

The sound of the ripping envelope was loud in the room. She unfolded the paper and two dark strips fell to the floor, misshapen leaves that shone in the anemic light from the hall. They were photographic negatives, four frames on each strip.

Just in case things go wrong, these are your insurance. I love you. Miguel. The words hurried across the unlined page. She dropped the paper and cried.

When she could, she leaned over, picking up the strips. She carried them to the gooseneck lamp and turned it on. When she held up the negatives, she could see a person coming toward the camera. Behind the figure, on the ground, lay a man. She stared through tear-washed eyes until the realization chilled her like a cold, slow draft: this must be the person who'd killed Judge Sarandon. The face was unrecognizable, its identifying features neutralized by the negative into bits of color, a code of light which she couldn't break. When had Miguel sent them?

The image of the words he'd written on the floor in his own blood flashed into her mind.

She started for the kitchen. The paper on the sofa fluttered with her own movement and she stopped short, staring at it as though it held danger. She again read her own name, this time in large, dramatic letters. Pulling the paper from the pin, she read the rest. *Call me as soon as you get home. Miguel was killed last night. Please let me help you. Elena.* Her phone number was scrawled under her name.

Tears filled Bianca's eyes. Yes, she would want to help her, but how could she? The policia had contacted her—how else could she know about Miguel? And they were probably watching her, because of the case in court—didn't they always watch the people who had come to their attention? she thought bitterly. If she went to Elena for help, they would take her, and if they didn't accuse her of killing Miguel, they would send her back to Mexico. She pressed her hand against her belly. Her baby would be raised in America.

OBSTACLE COURSE

She walked quickly to the kitchen, pulling open the cabinet door over the stove, rooting through the cans and bags for the sack of flour. A cockroach skittered under the shadow of her hand, a running watermelon seed seeking the dark. She dug into the flour, pulling out the small package wrapped in plastic, dusting it off against her skirt.

Her trembling fingers unfolded the paper and bills fell onto the counter. Fifty-four dollars. That was all.

She scrubbed the tears from her cheeks and looked again at the negatives. My insurance, she thought. He'd wanted equality, he'd gotten death. What had he thought she could do with them, these pictures of a murderer. Send them to the policia? They wouldn't help her. Elena could do nothing—look what had happened to her. Mrs. Garrett was deep in her own trouble.

The woman who had come to Mrs. Garrett's house. She wanted to help Mrs. Garrett. She had told her to call if she had any other information.

Bianca half ran to the tiny bathroom. She had thrown the woman's card into the wastebasket.

She dug out the card and let the wastebasket drop to the floor. FINNY ALETTER. 888-4746. No address. She ran back to the kitchen and grabbed for the phone book, leafing rapidly through the As. Here it was—

The rattle of the doorknob made her heart stop, then race into a tumbling rhythm. She snatched up the negatives and Finny's card, then forced the money into her pocket. A thud against the door sent her running out the back, holding the screen door to avoid its gunshot snap against the frame. She slipped down the alley.

Behind her in the kitchen the phone book sprawled open on the counter, its pages barely rippling at the opening of the unlocked front door.

Seventeen

THE TRAFFIC SIGNAL flashed green and Finny downshifted into first. She turned onto Eleventh, crossed Cherry Creek, flowing silent and shining beneath her, drove past the empty Rocky Mountain Bank Note building. Traffic was light; most intelligent people were home having dinner, thinking over their plans for the night. She had a more exciting life than that. She got to drive home wondering about a poor Mexican kid who was on the lam because her lover had been killed and she was afraid to go to the cops.

"Why do you suppose she didn't apply for amnesty?" Finny had asked Barelli before he left for police headquarters.

"If you'd been afraid of being kicked out of the country for the last six years, how willing would you be to go to the authorities, no matter how safe they told you it was?"

Finny saw his point. It'd be like hearing a school principal yell, "Olly-olly ox in free." Not bloody likely. Especially after she'd seen the system at work in Elena's case.

She turned into the alley beside her house, heard the splash of the tires in the water that streamed by in the gutter, saw the sprinklers at work next door. She'd better set out some of her own this evening.

The sun was just a memory now, and the evening cool was unfurling across the lawns and flower beds like fresh sheets spread on a mattress.

She was tired. The images that highlit this day should be put in a box and mailed on a slow boat to Bulgaria. If she hadn't gotten some new gray hairs from morning to dusk, then somewhere in the attic there had to be a portrait of her that looked like shit.

The automatic garage door opener worked its electronic magic, and she drove into the garage. She caught a glimpse of light from the kitchen window. Hmph. Chris must've beaten her home.

She levered herself out of the truck and went out the side door, shutting it firmly behind her. As she reached the middle of the yard, the kitchen light blinked off, leaving her in heavy shadow. Finny stopped, irritated. She hadn't turned on the yard light from the garage because she hadn't needed it with the kitchen light on. Damn the man. Sometimes he made the average absentminded professor look like a mental steel trap.

She made her way to the back door, grabbed the knob, and tried to open it. It was locked. Dammit, where was her house key? She shoved one hand into her jeans pocket. There.

The lock twisted and the door swung open to darkness. And suddenly something felt wrong. "Chris?"

She reached for the light switch just inside the door and her hand brushed against someone. Before the scream could leave her throat, she was hit hard in the gut. The air whooshed out of her and she doubled up, falling toward the floor. A large shape charged for the door, a heavy weight coming down hard on one of her feet as she fell. Through the ringing in her ears she heard the slam of the door, and then she did some serious concentrating on breathing.

A century or two later, Finny figured she was probably going to live. She'd be breathing shallowly for the next year or so, but she'd live. She struggled to a hands-and-knees position and made an attempt at standing up. The staying power in her legs would have made al dente spaghetti look like steel girders. If at first you don't succeed . . .

She ended up crawling across the floor to the wall with the light switch. She might have to spend the rest of her life hunched on the floor, but, by God, she wouldn't do it in the dark. Of course, that meant she had to get to her feet in order to turn on the light. Evolution must have felt like this.

Finny had just prepared herself for the ascent with a couple of careful breaths when the kitchen light went on, a bar of it shining through the door glass to the back porch.

"Finny?" Barelli's voice was urgent.

"Here," she croaked.

He pushed through the door. "Jesus." He surged across the porch to her and knelt at her side. "Are you all right?"

Before she could nod, he'd run his hands over her arms and legs and was peering into her eyes. "Can you move your hands, your feet?"

She complied and he pulled her up gently, swinging her up into his arms. "What the hell is going on here?" he growled. He strode into the kitchen and carried her on through the dining room to the sofa in the living room, where he set her down carefully. "Tell me what happened. Does it hurt anywhere?"

"Throw up," Finny managed and Barelli lunged for the wastebasket next to the couch. He braced her while she lost the remnants of their early dinner. "Sorry," Finny gasped after a short, nasty interlude.

"It's okay." Barelli grabbed a handful of tissues from the box on the coffee table and handed them to her. "You done?"

She nodded.

"I'll be right back." He eased her back into the sofa and carried out the wastebasket. When he came back he had a wet washcloth in one hand and a glass of water in the other. "Here, babe." He dabbed at her face with the washcloth and the coolness brought her back to life. "Take a sip of this." He held the water to her lips.

It helped.

"Can you talk now?"

"Yeah." When had she started sounding like Walter Brennan? She cleared her throat, wincing at the pain in her stomach muscles.

"What happened?"

She told him about the lights, the door being locked.

By the time she got to the monster who'd run over her, he was furious. "Didn't it occur to you that something weird was going on?"

"The whole damned day's been weird," Finny said. "I figured you'd gone out of the kitchen and turned off the light automatically. You do stuff like that all the time."

"Was it a man or a woman?"

"I don't know. He *or* she looked huge, but I was on the floor."

"Shit." Barelli glared at her. "You should never have come into the house after the lights went out. You have to use your instincts or you're dead meat."

"My instincts got bludgeoned today. Quit yelling at me."

He drew her against him carefully. "You scared me, dammit," he said above her ear. "When I saw the kitchen I thought you might have been attacked."

"What's wrong with the kitchen?" Finny nuzzled against the cool cotton of his shirt. Tears collected in her eyes.

"Looks like somebody was cooking up a storm—using the kitchen as the bowl."

Finny pulled back. "What?"

"Come see."

She let him pull her up and limped through the dining room, pushing on the swinging door to the kitchen. Inside was a disaster. The flour and sugar cannisters had been upended over the table and every cabinet door was open, giving a full view of dishes pushed hither and yon, of packages emptied, of piles of pasta, spices, everything. Papers, envelopes, and receipts were scattered like oversized confetti, and both volumes of the phone book sprawled debauchedly beside an empty baking powder tin. Several of the plants that screened the greenhouse windows overlooking the backyard lay amidst their pots, limp at the indignity. A small mound of coffee rested on the floor in front of the refrigerator, the emptied bag at its summit.

"Julia Child meets The Exorcist," Finny said in a thin voice. "I think I'll throw up again."

155

Barelli's gaze met hers. "Me first."

He went to the car for his kit, then dusted the doorknobs and plates and the glass of the back-door windows for fingerprints, but nothing showed up. "Either our friend wore gloves or wiped everything on the way out."

"Wonderful." Finny's gaze moved over the debris.

"I'll file a report tomorrow for insurance, but I don't see any reason to drag anybody over tonight."

Finny nodded. "There are advantages to having a cop around."

"Especially when it comes to picking up the pieces, right?"

Two hours later Finny's breathing still wasn't normal, but not because of the jab in the solar plexus. "I'd like to get my hands on whoever did this," she growled. "Strictly in the interest of rehabilitation, you understand."

Barelli glanced at the thick bottle of olive oil she brandished like a truncheon. "Yeah, you'd rehabilitate 'em right into next week." He twisted the tie around another garbage bag. "I wish I knew what the hell this is all about."

"Beats me." Finny grabbed the broom and swept the last of the comingled sugar and flour into the dustpan. She stood up wearily. "If whoever did this was looking for food, I'd sure as hell hate to see him eat it. He'd probably send Miss Manners into a coma."

Barelli picked up a head of lettuce that had been ripped nearly in half, then tossed it into the sink. "Looks like somebody was looking for something. I just wish I knew what." He hoisted two trash bags and headed out the back door.

Finny limped to one of the wicker chairs and sat down with a groan. "I think the son-of-a-bitch broke a couple of my toes," she said as he came back into the kitchen.

"You want to get them looked at?"

"What can they do for toes?"

"Not a hell of a lot." He went into the dining room and brought back the brandy bottle. "Here. I probably should've given you some earlier."

"I wouldn't have been able to keep it down, anyway."

Barelli got a couple of glasses out of the dishwasher and plunked them onto the table. "Knock some of this back and then it's bed."

"You know," Finny said. "This has been one of the crummiest days I've ever lived through."

Barelli rested his hand on her hair for an instant. "At least you're alive."

"Yeah." Finny forced the image of Michael Guiterrez's body out of her mind. She took another swallow of brandy. "Did you find out anything about Bianca Lopez?"

"No. There's no sign of her."

Finny blew out a breath. "Let's get some sleep. Tomorrow, as they say in the trade, is another day."

"Ain't it the truth." He pushed back his chair and held out one hand to tug her up. "You want me to carry you?"

"It's as big a thrill as you're going to get tonight."

He lifted her in his arms. "Be still my beating heart."

"Well," said Finny, "that, too."

Fixing breakfast the next morning didn't further Finny's quest for inner peace. Last night's prowler had emptied all the cereal boxes and had tossed more slices of bread around than a drunken baker. He or she apparently had no grudge against eggs, since they'd escaped the massacre. Finny scrambled the eggs, mourning the loss of her mocha almond coffee, a present she'd bought herself at FBC to the tune of $7.98 a pound. Damned philistine.

Barelli had lapsed into a brooding silence after he saw the purple circle on her stomach where the intruder had hit her. He was eating his breakfast with all the relish of an executioner working overtime, pretending to read the newspaper, sipping the herb tea she'd found intact, slanting a glance at her now and again.

"Chris, what is it?"

He let the paper rest on the table. "I want you to stop this thing."

"What thing?"

"The detective bit with Twee." His eyes met hers, and they were angry.

Finny's looked away. "You don't know that last night had anything to do with Twee."

"You don't know that it didn't." He pushed back the chair and stood up. "I don't like the feel of this, Finny. And I sure as hell don't like the idea of your poking around in this anymore. Not with Guiterrez dead, not with the asshole who punched you last night."

"Chris." Finny went to him, and he pulled her into his arms. "I'm okay, you know."

"Yeah, I know." He rested his chin on her head and his voice rumbled under her ear. "I'm going to talk to Bernie about reopening the Sarandon case. Guiterrez's murder has to make them want to take another look." He grasped her shoulders and pushed her far enough away to look into her eyes. "And I'd consider it a personal favor if you'd get back to building Corinne's linen closet."

Finny nodded slowly. "Okay. The only proviso is that you guys do open Twee's case again. If you don't, I can't make any promises, Chris."

His eyes narrowed as they met hers. After a moment, he nodded. "Fair enough."

It was definitely slow going this morning. Barelli had left for the wars a while ago and Finny was trying to get herself back into some kind of rhythm. She stood in the shower for a long time, struggling to think it through.

She'd managed to get her clothes on and her shoes tied before the phone issued a shrill summons. She picked up the receiver but, before she could say anything, the answering machine spiel clicked on. "You've reached 888-4746. At the tone, leave your name and number." She'd forgotten to turn on the delay switch last night.

"Finny, this is Abigail Hunter. The word's out that Twee is in the hospital. I want to know why and I want to know soon. Don't forget our deal. I haven't. Call me." By the sound of her, she could have advertised toothpaste: she was frothing at the mouth.

Finny hung up and headed for the stairs. She hadn't even checked for messages last night. It just hadn't occurred to her.

The answering machine's red light shone brightly and the first message was another missive of love from Abigail—marginally more polite than today's, but not by much.

The next message was from Les Trethalwyn. "Finny, I'm wondering if you could call me. I've found something interesting about our Mr. Engelman, and I think you'll be better for knowing it."

Finny dialed his number fast, then slammed down the receiver. Damn and blast. It was busy. She'd have to try again. Or she could go to his office and talk to him in person. The image of Barelli's face, grave, straightforward, trusting, flashed across her mind. And then she thought of Twee. Whatever she found out might help Twee. There was no guarantee that Les would talk to Barelli, was there? She could still serve as go-between until she heard that Denver's finest were back in harness, couldn't she?

She made a quick call to Corinne to explain her delay, then started hunting for her keys.

Eighteen

"—IN TOWN for tonight's premiere of Bizet's *Carmen* at the Denver Center for the Performing Arts. The performance, a benefit for the Serif Foundation has been sold—"

Finny pushed the radio button and the driving beat of the Stones filled the cab of her pickup. A little down-and-dirty suited her mood.

A Trans-Am pulled out of a parking place as she passed the huge Dave Cook's store, and she darted for it like a hungry trout lunges for a fly. She locked the doors and headed up the mall toward Larimer Street.

Sunshine was falling on Writer Square as she rounded the corner onto Larimer, bathing the red brick of the buildings and the walks. Across the street, the copper pots in the window of Williams-Sonoma gleamed without the benefit of the sun. Finny strode past the shops, past the Market, breathing in the perfume of strong, dark coffee that wafted from the open doorway, seeking and finding the discreet brass plaque posted on the white painted wood next to a doorway squeezed between two shops.

The Denver Arts Consortium was on the second floor, Suite 201. The stairs were soft with gray carpeting, and the promise in the scent of fresh paint and furniture wax was fulfilled in the small, sleek reception area that extended like a living room at the top.

Danish modern chairs in blond wood and a soft blue and violet plaid upholstery lounged coolly around the clean lines of the birch table that held copies of *Premiere* and

Interview, Muse and *Variety*. If one could extrapolate from the decor, the Consortium was doing all right.

The soft, hurried music of a muted telephone bell played in the background—another layer in the patina of success. The sleek receptionist glanced up to give Finny the once-over with the speed of a grocery store scanner. The woman was savvy, and she didn't have any time to waste.

"May I help you?" The delivery was business straight up, the accent pure London.

Finny smiled. "Yes. I need to talk—"

The door to the right of the desk opened and Les Trethalwyn looked around the edge of it. "Sarah, do be a love—" He stopped short. "Miss Aletter—Finny. Just the person I've wanted to see."

"Les." She stepped forward to clasp the hand he extended. "I tried to get through by phone, but—" She glanced back at the secretary who was picking up the receiver yet again.

Trethalwyn moved back and motioned Finny through the door to his office. "It's a madhouse today. *Carmen* premieres tonight, you know, and last-minute panic has set in." He waved her into a gray leather chair, skirted the Queen Anne table that served as a desk to his own chair, and sat. "It's good of you to come here."

"I couldn't ignore your message. What have you found out?"

Trethalwyn leaned back in his chair. In his white shirt and striped tie, his curling hair brushed back from his forehead, he looked the normal businessman, but his dancing brown eyes played against the staid image. "Would it surprise you to know that dear Ty Engelman is on the brink of bankruptcy?"

Finny's forehead creased in a frown. "I'd have expected money problems, but I'm surprised he's that bad off. How do you know?"

"I have my sources." His smile was satisfied with her reaction. "Ty's been seen a great deal on the social scene during the last year or so—at the benefits and many of the parties. And that's an expensive pastime."

"Yes, I know that." Finny looked across the desk at him, puzzled. "So?"

"It occurred to me to check into his financial standing. Since he hangs about Paige Dexter a great deal, I wondered if Paige has been subsidizing him all along. He has to have some source of funds."

"So you're speculating that he could've had money—through Paige—as a motive for killing Sarandon. Rather obvious, isn't it?"

"Perhaps." Trethalwyn folded his hands together on the shining desktop. "But I can't help thinking that marriage to Paige would solve his problems."

"Why opt for murder when a divorce was in the offing?" Finny asked.

"Ah, but was it?" Trethalwyn nodded at Finny's look of surprise. "Paige and William had been separated for a long, long time—so long that some questioned whether a divorce would ever happen. And I wonder if Paige would get quite as healthy a settlement—not to mention any sort of bequest in William's will."

Finny thought of the way Ty had acted around Paige: attentive, even possessive. "It seems a bit shortsighted to commit murder without having sewn up his position. That is, if, as you suggest, Paige and William both were stalling the divorce."

Les raised his hands in a who-knows gesture. "It seems worthy of attention to me."

"Certainly." Finny was thinking back to the evening of the party. How would the timing have worked, putting Ty into the murderer's role? She'd encountered him after she left Twee, but before she ran into Judge Sarandon. She'd seen him with Paige after Sarandon's body was discovered, but that was all.

Finny shook her head. "I don't know. It's possible, I suppose, but it'll take more than his being broke to make a case for his murdering Sarandon."

"Oh, indeed," said Trethalwyn quickly. "Such as his feelings for Paige. And perhaps hers for him." His slightly inquiring tone brought Finny's eyes up to his. "Far be it for me to malign the lady, but it does seem to me that she's tried to be very much the fence sitter in regards to Ty Engelman."

"One could get that impression," Finny said slowly. She was remembering the come-hither look Paige gave Ty at Twee's. But she hadn't been that glad to see him the day of the luncheon.

"I just thought you ought to be made cognizant of what I'd discovered," Les said. He rose from his chair and came around his desk. "You know how much I want to help Twee."

"Yes, of course." Finny rose and extended her hand. "You've given me something to think about."

"Just trying to bring possibilities to your attention." Les opened his office door and escorted her through.

"Mr. Trethalwyn," began his secretary, "there's a call from Mrs. Travis on line two. Can you take it?"

"I suppose I'd better deal with the estimable Mrs. Travis."

"Good-bye," Finny said. "Thanks."

He raised his hand in a wave and went back into his office.

Finny went down the stairs thoughtfully. Everything Les had told her pointed to Ty.

Finny pushed the door open and emerged onto the sidewalk, now filling with knots of people moving like bloodclots through the larger currents of humanity streaming past the shops. If what Les was suggesting was true, if Ty had been the one to kill William Sarandon, then had he also killed Michael Guiterrez?

She reached her truck, unlocked the door, and climbed in. What if Michael Guiterrez happened to snap a couple of pictures of Ty doing in the judge? Or, for that matter, Paige doing the dirty deed? Then there'd be an enormous connection among all of them—all class barriers aside.

The niggling worry at this point was, why was Les Trethalwyn working so hard to hang the judge's murder on Ty? He was a busy man, but he'd taken the time to research Ty's finances. It was enough to make her wonder about Les's motives.

The traffic was thickening into the lunchtime lunacy

when Finny steered her little pickup into the fray. What she ought to do now was head straight to Corinne's house for an intensive bout of sanding. She flicked on the signal light and veered into the exit for the Valley Highway. What she was going to do was try one more angle before she hung up her curiosity.

Finny swept onto the Belleview exit. Cuffy hadn't told her much—certainly not enough—but she had the outstanding virtue of knowing all the players in the drama. At this point in the mish-mash of the last week, that was the only advantage to be had.

Finny pulled through the wagon-wheel gate and parked in front of Cuffy's house. If this was going to be her last shot, she'd make it count.

She rapped sharply on the door and, a moment later, it opened.

"Finny?" In her faded jeans and t-shirt, her copper hair caught into a ponytail over each ear, Cuffy Sarandon looked about fifteen. "What are you doing here?"

"I've come to ask a favor—two, really. May I come in?"

"Sure." Cuffy stepped aside. "What is it you want?"

Finny ran a hand through her hair. "I want you to get me into your father's house."

"Now, wait a minute—"

Finny held up one hand. "Hear me out."

Cuffy turned away. "Come into the kitchen," she said brusquely. "I was just getting a drink."

Finny trailed after her, took the glass of lemonade Cuffy proffered, and drank the tart, cold liquid gratefully. "Thanks."

"All right," Cuffy said. "Tell me what this is about."

"You're father was not a popular man," Finny said. "The Parmetter case, as well as others, made a lot of people hate him. Then there was the Jericho Mountain deal."

"So?" Cuffy set her glass down with a firm tap. "You're not telling me anything I don't already know."

"It occurred to me that there might be other reasons for people to have a grudge against him. He was on the bench for quite a while, and I've heard people say there were other business deals."

"My father was a businessman *and* a judge," Cuffy said shortly. "Of course there were other deals, and other people involved with them. That doesn't change the fact that Twee has confessed to killing him."

"Cuffy, please." Finny started to touch her arm, then changed her mind at the expression of distaste that crossed the woman's face. "If you have any feeling for Twee, let me at least check. The police didn't finish going through his effects because Twee confessed. There might be something that would help her."

Cuffy was shaking her head. "You are incredible. Loyal to the end."

Finny wanted to smack the cool amusement off her face. "What's the matter, don't you think people in my class are capable of loyalty?"

"Your class?" Cuffy's eyes smouldered. "Finny, you're such a snob. Always on the lookout for a putdown, always quick to grasp at the differences. You're no better than people like my mother."

"That's bullshit and you know it."

"No, I don't know it. I've spent half my life listening to people like you, the ones who're convinced that, because I have money, I come from another species. You're no different."

Finny stared at her. She supposed that she did resent the wealth, the position. And how odd, because she didn't really want to be a part of that world. It wasn't that she didn't have the framework of either wealth or family. She just figured she'd be bored. So why the edge, why the sarcasm? "You might be right," Finny said on a rueful note. "Jesus, you might just be right."

Cuffy seemed to lose momentum, a balloon deflated on the edge of flight. "What?"

"I have been looking at this whole thing as though all the players came from another planet," Finny said in a low voice. "All I could see was Twee doing the noblesse oblige bit. But what if that isn't it at all?"

"So, what else could it be?" Cuffy had put her hands

on her hips, her head cocked in curiosity like a considering child. "Except for being the murderer, why else would she confess?"

"I'm not sure, but I think it was because she really wanted to, and she feels guilty that she didn't." Finny looked up from the floor, into Cuffy's face. "I need a favor—I need you to get me into your father's house. I haven't told anybody about you and Kit, so, if you want to get technical about it, you owe me."

"Owe you? For what? You never—"

"All right, then you owe Twee. Just do it, Cuffy. Trust me, okay?"

Cuffy stared at her measuringly, then nodded. "Okay, I'll do it. But, so help me, Finny, if you cross me . . ."

"Shit, what am I going to do?" Finny watched her as she swept up a handbag and started for the door. "I already perjured my soul with Abigail Hunter, and if that doesn't prove I'm trustworthy, I don't know what does."

Cuffy stopped, her hand on the doorknob. "Finny, this doesn't have anything to do with my mother, does it?"

Just for a moment Finny considered lying to her. That was when she finally accepted Cuffy for what she was. "It might," she said flatly. "I don't know."

Cuffy's eyes met hers squarely. "Let's go," she said gruffly, then slammed the door behind them.

TRIP WIRE

"THAT'LL BE four forty-three." The Foto-Tek clerk glanced over her shoulder impatiently at the continuing shriek of the telephone. The ends of her long brown ponytail caught on her name tag, obscuring the "Joan" scrawled in crooked letters. "Dammit," she muttered, then, "Sammy, can you get the phone?"

Bianca sorted slowly through the small bunch of bills in her wallet and pulled out a worn five.

The girl took it from her and hurriedly punched numbers into the cash register. The drawer slid open and she scooped coins out of the dividers. "Forty-four, forty-five, fifty and five." She pushed the packet of photographs toward Bianca and stretched her red, full lips in a smile. "Thanks. You come back, now."

The bell on the glass door jingled as Bianca opened it and went out into the hot, heavy air of late afternoon. Clouds were gathering over the mountains like members of an angry mob.

She barely glanced at the package in her hand. She wanted to sit down first. Waves of fatigue were making her dizzy, and the coffee and roll she'd eaten at the little café near the bus station were lying on her stomach like the bad memories in her mind.

She walked down the sidewalk until she saw the tables outside Hummel's. She sat in one of the metal chairs and watched the aproned young waitress come toward her. "Ice tea," she murmured. She shouldn't spend the money, but she couldn't walk any further right now, no matter what.

The girl set a tall, thick glass in front of her, and Bianca reached for it greedily. The cold, quenching liquid slid down her dry throat, the ice cubes in it pushing against her lips.

She could put it off no longer. She picked up the envelope of photographs and fumbled with the flap that sealed it closed. The paper tore and she widened the opening. When she turned the packet upside down, eight squares fell out onto the table top.

Deborah turned them over, one by one, thinking of her grandfather, playing his card games in the village bodega with Señor Gonzales.

The first picture was a blend of blacks and grays and whites and she could make no sense of it. The shapes were ill-defined. The second picture was the same and her eyes filled with bitter tears. *These* were what Miguel had died for?

Her hand was trembling as she turned over the

third square, and when she saw what was on it her breath caught in her throat. As if moving under its own power, her hand turned over the other photographs, each one more damning than the last. *Madre de Dio.* Miguel must have gone back after the Judge had pawed at her and seen what had happened. He had taken pictures of the judge and his murderer. Miguel had thought to gain the things they didn't have with these pieces of filth.

She was swept with an enormous rage. The father of her child was dead and this, this *cabron* was responsible. She gathered the photos together in an abrupt movement and stuffed them back into their envelope. What was she supposed to do with these? Miguel had called them her insurance. If she tried to use them she would end up as dead as he was.

Bianca stared at the envelope. In the moment of quiet she could almost hear Miguel's voice. "They don't know you're alive. You're a part of the furniture." Tears stung at her eyes and the hand that held the envelope tightened. Rage flowed through her. This one would know she was alive. She would make sure of that.

Nineteen

CONVERSATION WAS as sparse as dandruff on a bald man during the drive to Judge Sarandon's house.

At Cuffy's curt instruction, Finny steered her pickup onto Williams, through a brick gate. She'd never seen the houses here, nestled on the hill above the Denver Country Club. The thick growth of trees and the elegant and forbidding fence on Alameda hardly encouraged sightseeing.

The street wound gently to the right, through a mini-forest of pines and aspens, curving eventually in front of a house that looked as though it had grown up from the soil, its stone walls an almost-pink support for the Virginia creeper that clung lovingly to it. Peeking above a youthful Scotch pine was an eyebrow window in the broach roof. A bay window at the east side of the house fronted on a stand of Douglas spruces, where a colony of sparrows twittered over the happenings of the day.

Finny took in the perfection of the scene glumly. If I see a lion sunbathing with a lamb, I'm out of here, she thought.

"Don't stop," Cuffy hissed suddenly, and Finny caught sight of a dark green fender at the west side of the house.

Finny obligingly kept her foot on the accelerator and continued along the narrow street that curved through the area. "What's up?" she asked.

"That was my mother's car."

"You sure?"

Cuffy glanced at her. "How many license plates say 'DareCare'?"

"Point made." Finny braked as they came to the next house. "What now?"

Cuffy shrugged. "Why ask me? I'm just along for the ride."

Finny considered her for a moment. "Why would your mother be at your father's house?"

"God knows." Cuffy raised a shoulder in a half-hearted shrug. "Estate details?"

"Who's the executor of your father's estate?"

"MacKenzie Bartholomew."

"You're kidding."

Cuffy lifted a brow at the note of surprise in Finny's voice. "Why shouldn't he be? He and my father knew each other for at least a hundred years."

"He's also Twee's lawyer. Doesn't that strike you as just a tad murky, conflict-of-interest-wise?"

"Not necessarily." Cuffy sounded belligerent. "Mac knows everybody who's anybody. He's probably worked for three-quarters of the people I know."

Finny's lips twisted. "Is he your lawyer, too?"

"I don't need one." Cuffy shifted impatiently. "Look, are we going to hang around here all day? I've got other things to do."

"Sorry." Finny stared out the windshield. She hated like hell to waste the drive over. Turning off the engine, she opened her door. "Let's go."

Cuffy was watching her with suspicion. "Go where?"

"To your father's house." Finny shut the door and waited for Cuffy to slide out the other side. "We'll walk back and see what we can see."

"You want to peek through the windows?"

"What d'you think we'd see?" Finny met the anger in Cuffy's eyes. "I've got other things to do, too. Now, do you want to try and figure out Twee's part in this, or not?"

Cuffy's eyes clouded. "I don't know. Dammit, I just don't know."

Gored on the horns of a dilemma. Finny gestured her forward.

They walked back to Judge Sarandon's house, Cuffy slightly in the lead. Finny's rubber-soled shoes were silent on the fresh black asphalt; the heels of Cuffy's riding boots thudded in brisk cadence.

"The driveway's just past the corner." Cuffy glanced over her shoulder. "What do you want to do?"

"Let's go around back." Finny stepped off the sidewalk. Trees were bunched like conversation groups, and she could see the dark green of Paige's car through the spaces among them.

Silent, they threaded their way through the trees. They came to the edge of the emerald carpet of grass that surrounded William Sarandon's house. At a sound Finny caught at Cuffy's arm. "Wait a minute," she whispered.

Across the greensward, from behind the house, they saw a figure heading toward the car. It was Paige stalking toward the Mercedes as if she were planning to destroy it.

There was a sharp sound, then Ty Engelman shot around the corner of the house as if he'd been catapulted from it. "Paige," he called loudly. "Wait."

Paige moved on as if she hadn't heard. She reached the side of the car and wrenched open the door. Ty ran to her, grabbing her by one arm before she could get into the car.

"What's going—" Cuffy started, then stopped at the pressure on her shoulder.

Paige had pulled her arm from Ty's grasp, facing him, talking rapidly. Finny strained to hear what she was saying, but she couldn't make it out. From the body language, though, Paige was verbally slicing Ty into julienne strips. When she lifted one hand and slapped Ty across the face, Cuffy gasped. "My God—"

Ty stood still. Paige said something else to him, then brushed past him toward the car. Ty jerked around and caught hold of her arm. "Let go of me," Finny and Cuffy heard her demand. Then Ty hauled off and slapped her.

Cuffy took a step forward, but Finny held her back. "Wait."

Paige had held one hand to her cheek, staring up at Ty as if she'd never seen him before. Then she melted toward him, pressing against him. He bent his head to kiss her and Paige's fingers slid up his shoulders into his hair, her frantic mouth twisting underneath his. Ty swung her up in his arms, their mouths still joined, then carried her toward the house.

Finny didn't meet Cuffy's eyes. "Let's get out of here."

Cuffy turned on her heel and started back to the pickup.

Finny slid the key into the lock and listened for a moment after the door had swung open. What Barelli had said about her not using her instincts the night before had registered. He'd be so pleased. Especially if he found out about her abortive attempt to case Judge Sarandon's house.

Her own house held an air of empty waiting. Which beat the hell out some of the alternatives.

She locked the door behind her and leaned against it for a minute. The journey back to Cuffy's house had been silent and awkward. Finny had remembered an article she'd once read about sexuality: children, no matter what their ages, could never comfortably accept the idea that their parents actually engaged in the evil act. Cuffy obviously was having a hard time with some of the messier details of Paige's personal relationships. Finny hadn't been too thrilled about seeing behind the veneer herself. Somehow the notion of Paige, lacquered and superior, getting off on violence did not appeal.

Finny sighed, pushing herself toward the living room. She was tired, and she felt dirty from spying on people. She dropped her keys onto the round oak coffee table and glanced toward the answering machine. Its flashing red light winked at her provocatively. More grist for the mill, no doubt. She was more than a little sick of the whole thing—this good deed she'd set out to do. She'd stirred up the stewpot and wasn't liking what had risen to the top. Why didn't she just face the truth that Twee didn't want to be saved and go back to her thrilling life of creative carpentry?

Because I'm an incurable buttinsky, she pointed out to herself. Because I hate like hell for things not to work out right. A case of arrested development, stuck at the fairy tale level: and everyone lived happily ever after. Bullshit.

She rewound the tape and turned it on. Woody Jordan's

deep-in-the-heart-of-Texas voice poured into the air, as thick as gravy.

"Finny, honey, regardin' our little talk the other day, I tripped over some information you might want to think about. Call me just as soon as you can." He recited both business and home phone numbers.

As soon as she heard the beep indicating the end of the message, Finny turned off the machine and started punching in numbers. When Woody answered his office number after five rings, Finny relaxed a little. "I got your message," she said, sinking onto the sofa. "What's up?"

"I didn't think a whole lot about our talk the other day," Woody said. "But yesterday I had lunch with an old friend of mine, one who keeps his ear close to the ground. He mentioned Ty Engelman and I thought you might want to hear what he said."

"Sure I do," Finny said. "What happened to your accent, Woody?"

"I hang it up after working hours." He sounded tired. "You want the info or not?"

"Go on." Finny levered one shoe off, then the other.

"Engelman was trying to put together a land deal. He'd been pitching it to a number of people until all his financing fell apart. Word has it that William Sarandon put the kibosh on the deal."

Finny shivered. "Who else was involved, Woody? Did you get any other names?"

His raspy voice got even lower. "Keep in mind that I barely got Sarandon's, but there were a couple more, or at least rumors of 'em. One's Alden Morrison, the other's Les Trethalwyn. All of 'em took a bath in red ink."

"What?" Finny's hand was tight on the receiver. "Les Trethalwyn?"

"Don't you know him? He's a Brit—works for the Arts—"

"I know him." Finny remembered the friendly smile Les had given her that morning. "He was involved?"

"He was on the list of investors."

"Woody, why would Sarandon do that to Ty?"

Woody's chuckle sounded like dried cornhusks rubbing

together. "Finny, it's as basic as A-B-C: a case of money and women. Ol' Ty's been sniffin' around Paige Dexter for a while. Almost as long as Les Trethalwyn. I guess ol' William thought he'd get rid of both men. Paige always has had money, and she wouldn't look at anybody who didn't have it or wasn't about to get it."

Finny's head was spinning with possibilities. Les. Maybe he'd thought to kill two birds with one stone, too. He'd been so eager to pass on the dirt about Ty. Of course, it made perfect sense. He'd done it all along, starting with that first phone call. Pointing her in Ty's direction, he'd carefully fed her information to keep her suspicions growing. That had been some performance this morning. Now that she thought about it, Les and Paige had seemed fairly friendly the night of Twee's party.

"Finny?"

"What?"

"I've gotta get going. It's my culture night."

"The Broncos don't start playing again till August, Woody."

"Very funny. I'll have you know I've had season tickets to the opera for many a year. And I got me a cute little redhead waitin' for the steak I promised her."

"Okay, okay, I'm impressed." She paused. "Woody? Thanks—I owe you."

"I still drink Chivas, darlin'. Take care."

Finny replaced the receiver. Oh, things were getting interesting. If Les was setting up Ty, then things were getting very interesting indeed.

She pressed the playback button again. The tape whirred, then began to speak. "Finny, it's Corinne Danovich. Please call me." She sounded very prim and disapproving.

Finny flicked off the message switch and punched in Corinne's number. The poor woman probably wants to fire me, she thought guiltily.

"Hello?"

"Corinne? It's Finny."

"Oh, I'm so glad you called. I was beginning to be afraid you'd get back too late."

"Too late for what?"

"I have a favor to ask," Corinne went on in businesslike fashion. "I have season tickets to the opera and tonight is the opening, as you probably know."

"Yes?"

"I always attend with my friend Louise, but she's in Galveston with her first grandchild, who was born this morning. Would you like to use her ticket? I'd really enjoy your company."

Finny blinked. "Uh, you mean tonight?"

"Yes. The premiere is this evening at eight o'clock."

Irony is at work, Finny thought. Why the hell not? She'd probably see Les Trethalwyn there. She could ask him if he'd killed Sarandon during the intermission. It would be *the* event of the season.

"Okay. I'd be happy to drive. What time should I pick you up?"

"Well, very soon," Corinne said apologetically. "That is, if you want to have time to get something to eat. And Finny," awkwardly, "it *is* a premiere. I'm wearing a long dress, but do feel free to wear whatever you like. Some people go to extremes as far as dress is concerned, but the range is from formal to informal to eccentric. Whatever you decide is fine with me."

"Thanks, Corinne." The poor woman had never seen her in anything but jeans and t-shirts. "I'll be there as soon as I can."

Twenty

THE DENVER CENTER for the Performing Arts was sprawling, multileveled, the straight, harsh lines of its concrete walls softened by archways of glass. Flights of stairs and pipe railings zigzagged in geometric whimsy up, down, and across the impassive gray slabs that formed it. Tonight the lights were bright, casting shadows of the people who moved toward glass doors in streams, refracting into glitters off jewelry of gold and precious stones, gleaming dully from rich fabrics of gowns and tuxedos, highlighting hair that had been carefully crafted into curls and waves. Anticipation rode a vagrant breeze like perfume through the molten patterns of the gathering crowd as they moved toward the Boettcher Concert Hall.

Finny walked beside Corinne, unobtrusively shielding her from the momentum of the crush. Looking dignified in a plain black taffeta dress, its severe bodice covered by a short matching jacket, Corinne proceeded in stately fashion. From the smoothly braided coronet to the gold and jet earrings dancing against flushed cheeks, she was clearly afloat on the excitement of the evening. She had met Finny at the door, eager to be underway, smiling her approval at Finny's outfit.

She'd thrown herself into a deep orange cotton sundress, figuring that, with the long circle skirt that swirled around her legs, and the brown strappy heels, she'd at least look somewhat dressy. The oversized gold-rust-brown paisley scarf she wrapped around her bare shoulders deepened her tan and highlighted her black hair. Gold hoops at her ears added to the gypsy effect—surely acceptable for *Carmen*.

There hadn't been much time to primp. As soon as she'd gotten off the phone with Corinne she'd checked through the rest of the answering machine's messages. Chris's call had been the last.

"Gotta work late, babe. The lab boys came up with a couple of latent prints in the Guiterrez killing and we got somebody who saw a car outside Guiterrez's building. Anyway, I'll see you when I see you."

Finny tried a quick call to headquarters, but Barelli wasn't there. A glance at the clock dictated that she write him a note and hope for the best. If she didn't get out to Corinne's, her ass was grass.

Once through the revolving glass door, Finny and Corinne were pressed into the mass milling outside the concert hall doors. The foyer repeated the modern lines of the building's exterior, the carpeted floors easing against more concrete walls soaring upward. A long stairway leading to a second level where the upper tier seats were located was gorged with dresses and suits making their way upward. Waves of sound accompanied them as opera goers found one another and exchanged greetings, their gusts and trills of laughter, soprano to basso profundo, bubbling through the buzz of conversation like birdsong.

"We go this way." Corinne had led the way past the stairway and was serenely dodging bodies as she headed into a passage that circled the round stage inside the concert hall. The tunnel-like approach widened into a small gallery, its walls sporting etchings and paintings. Moderately sized sculpture stood about like hesitant visitors.

Finny fought back nascent claustrophobia as they went through the passage, wincing as she caught sight of a painting that portrayed an anorexic figure on a scaffold. Just the sort of art to have hanging around for an opera about murder.

As they entered through wide doors into the concert hall, Finny glanced around, hoping to catch sight of Les Trethalwyn. For what, she wasn't quite sure. She'd gone from thinking of him as a solid citizen to wondering if he were a murderer. Maybe she wanted to see if he looked any different, as if that would help her decide.

It was impossible to find anyone in the large, circular room. Tiers of chairs extended up the walls behind the theater seats on the floor around the stage. The high backs of the far seats framed the people sitting in them, creating an oddly formal effect.

"Here we are." Corinne preceded Finny to their seats, several rows back from the platform stage in the round.

Finny pardoned herself past several sets of knees and sank to her seat.

"I do wish I'd had one more ticket for your lieutenant," Corinne said.

"Remember? He had to work late."

Finny recognized MacKenzie Bartholomew several rows in front of her. He was splendid in a dark suit, bending with old-fashioned courtesy over the person seated next to him. His wife, perhaps? But she couldn't even see if it was a man or a woman thanks to the people seated between them. Her gaze skipped across the orchestra pit to the woman in a Scarlett O'Hara gown, crinolines and all.

"There she is," Corinne hissed.

Finny jerked her head round. "Who?"

"Emeline Hanratty."

Following the direction of her admiration, Finny looked down the row. The glowing aura of mauve was unmistakable, rising from hair that had been marcelled into waves of astonishing complexity. Emeline had, if anything, increased the intensity of the rinse she used, and the color clashed impressively with the cloth-of-gold dress that hung stiffly around her. She lowered her body to a sitting position in ceremonial style and Corinne sighed. "Doesn't she look wonderful?"

Finny contented herself with a vague sound. Corinne definitely had a thing about dear old Emeline.

She scanned the program, startled to find Twee's name at the front. *With deep thanks for all her efforts on behalf of the Denver Arts Consortium, the premiere of* Carmen *is dedicated to Twee Garrett*. Finny closed the booklet. Les must have been responsible for that. He really did like Twee.

At the initial tunings of the orchestra, the conversational hum in the room first increased, then began to die. The lights came up on the stark structures of the set and the auditorium lights dimmed slowly.

The conductor walked to his podium to the spatter of applause. After a quick glance at his score he lifted his baton and the overture began.

Finny relaxed, letting her gaze wander over the audience. Behind her she could hear someone whispering but soon the soft rustling noise died away and she drifted into the music of *Carmen*. She surfaced briefly to cough when the cigarette girls filed onto the stage, all of them smoking like locomotives, then succumbed once again to the magic. Don José was magnetic, his acting as good as his voice, and Carmen flamed. Not even the simultaneous and sometimes strange translations in lighted displays on either side of the stage could distract her.

As the house lights came up, Finny returned to the present with a start. She had thought to come up with some kind of plan to find Les. So much for good intentions.

Corinne was on her feet and determinedly making her way toward the aisle. "Come on, Finny," she said impatiently. "If you want something to drink, we've got to get out there."

The Broncos should have hired her, Finny thought. The rapid path Corinne blazed through the less-decided members of the audience would have translated well into broken field running—particularly after they lost the smokers who had slowed to pull out cigarettes, pipes, and cigars with frenzied speed.

Corinne couldn't quite belly up to the bar—she was too short—but that didn't impede her effectiveness. "Finny?"

"Uh, white wine."

Corinne turned back to the bartender and Finny watched as the rest of the thundering herd caught up with them. Abigail Hunter, flanked by both men and women, was walking through the mob as if she were on a stroll through the park, heading straight for her. Before Finny could cut and run, Abigail had seen her and was on her way.

Smiling brilliantly, stunning in black silk, Abigail approached for a social kiss. "I'm going to hold you by the heels over an open fire." She whispered in Finny's ear. She pulled back and announced that she wanted scotch, straight up.

While several of her entourage scurried to fulfill her wishes, she glared at Finny. "You made a deal with me, and you haven't paid off. Do you know what I could do to you?"

Corinne was looking up at Finny anxiously. "Is anything wrong?"

"No, it's all right, Corinne." Finny grabbed Abigail by the arm and tugged her away from the clutch of listeners at the bar. "Listen, there's more at stake here than your damned column. It's called a murder investigation, and until it's over, you'll have to wait for your scoop."

"I won't wait forever, I'll tell you that." She was scrabbling through her tiny purse for cigarettes, finally pulling a small gold case from it.

Before she could find matches, a large hand holding a cocked platinum lighter presented itself in front of her. "You need a light, ma'am?"

"Woody?"

He flashed a smile down at Finny. Resplendent in a tux, restraining his individuality to burgundy bow tie and cummerbund, he winked and turned back to Abigail. "I don't believe we've been introduced," he drawled. Abigail straightened, lifting her chin just a little.

Finny edged away. Saved.

She and Corinne had nearly finished their drinks when Woody found them. He grabbed Finny by both shoulders for a French salute. "You didn't tell me you were coming tonight." He beamed down at her, flushed with pleasure, especially his nose, which glowed with a life of its own under limpid blue eyes. His thick gray hair fell over his forehead. "Last time I paid attention, your definition of a good time involved paint or manure, maybe both."

"You can't insult me, Woody. I'm too grateful for being rescued."

"From that young flower of womanhood?" Woody grinned. "I'm meeting her for a drink after the fat lady sings."

"Watch your back."

The end of intermission signal chimed, calling them back to their seats. Finny waggled her fingers at Woody, venturing forth ahead of Corinne. This time *she* could protect *her*.

They were nearly to the stairs when Finny glimpsed Ty and Paige. Apparently all pretense at mourning was at an end. Blooming in a vivid red cocktail dress, Paige was holding Ty's arm tightly. He moved beside her with assurance, guiding her smoothly. Nice contrast to the all-star wrestling bit that afternoon, Finny thought dryly. Somebody somewhere would undoubtedly say they'd been the making of each other.

Paige's glance crossed Finny's and she stiffened. Ty looked down at her, then raised his eyes to find Finny. They both turned their heads away with the precision of a drill team, sweeping up the carpeted stairs.

"They're a blatant pair, the two of them."

Finny swung around, her heart pounding at the cadence of the accent. Les Trethalwyn observed the departing couple, bitterness in his eyes, his jaw tensed.

"You seem angry," Finny said softly.

He stared after them. "She's a bitch, you know. She wouldn't know real emotion if she tripped over it."

"She seemed upset at Judge Sarandon's death."

Les snorted. "Bloody hell."

"Were you a close friend of William Sarandon's?" Finny watched him expressionlessly.

"No, not close." Les glanced around. "Don't you think you'd better get back to your seat?"

The foyer was nearly empty. "I guess I'd better. Shall I see you later?"

Les nodded. "I'll look for you."

The music had already begun when Finny found her

way back to her seat. "What happened?" Corinne whispered.

"Nothing, I just saw someone." She settled in for the second act. As always, things were not going well for Don José.

The spell had been broken. Finny found her thoughts straying to Les Trethalwyn. Could he have had an affair with Paige Dexter? From what Woody said, it wouldn't be outside the realm of possibilities. That could explain Les's bitterness. And, possibly, why he kept trying to implicate Ty in Sarandon's death. What better way to get rid of a rival than to have him charged with murder? Especially after you'd gotten rid of an inconvenient husband yourself for helping you lose your money. Revenge à la mode.

The stage lights brightened for the scenery change before the third act. Finny had just turned to Corinne when she saw MacKenzie Bartholomew helping his companion up the aisle. His arm was tightly around the woman's shoulders and she leaned on him heavily. They were nearly even with Finny's row when she realized that the woman was Twee Garrett.

"My God!" She got to her feet and followed the two of them out, barely aware of Corinne's startled question.

It didn't take long to catch up with them. Twee was walking very slowly, each step an effort.

"Good evening." Finny spoke quietly. "Could you use some help?"

Twee looked blankly into her face, not recognizing her. "A shadow game," she mumbled thickly. She was struggling for breath. "Always look for the silent partners."

Finny put her arm around Twee's back in support. "Goddammit," she said sotto voce to MacKenzie Bartholomew. "What kind of insanity made you bring her here? How'd she get out of the hospital?"

Bartholomew's forehead was dotted with sweat; he was supporting most of Twee's weight. "I couldn't dissuade her. She said she'd started all this and she was going to finish it."

"Let's get her to the lounge."

By the time they reached the women's rest room, Twee

was gasping, her face gray. "Help me get her inside. I think there's a bench or something."

"But—" Bartholomew gestured at the LADIES sign.

"Fuck that," Finny growled. "Help me."

They half carried Twee inside, easing her down onto the shiny vinyl sofa outside the lavatory. Finny caught a glimpse of the attendant's black uniform in the other room. "You'd better phone for an ambulance," she told Bartholomew. He stood looking at Twee as if he hadn't heard her.

"Dammit, go call for help!"

Bartholomew stumbled from the door out to the hall.

"Can you bring me a towel?" Finny called to the attendant.

She heard the rustle of the uniform and held out her hand, her gaze on Twee's face. If anything, she'd become even paler, and her breathing was fast and shallow. When she had the cool cloth on her hand, Finny put the towel across Twee's forehead.

"You'll be all right, Twee," Finny was saying in a low voice. "Take it easy now, you'll be fine. An ambulance will be here soon. Just relax."

Twee's eyes opened and she looked into Finny's face. "I'm perfectly fine," she said. "Don't worry."

"That's my girl." Finny had to force the words past the lump in her throat. "Keep fighting."

"You know, Finny," Twee's eyes closed for a moment, then reopened. "Paige should have ordered the gazebo. It would have been quite striking."

"It's okay, Twee. Don't worry about it. Could you make sure the ambulance is on its way?" Finny said over her shoulder to the attendant. There was no answer and, after a quick glance over the room, Finny realized that no one was there.

"I'm sorry, Herbert," Twee said quite clearly. "It never occurred to me that he was involved." Her eyes closed.

"Oh, God." Finny bent over her. "Twee, hold on. Don't die on me, Twee."

Twee exhaled on a long sigh, and Finny's heart nearly

stopped. Then she took a short, jerky breath and began to breathe normally. "You were right, Finny."

Dammit, where was the ambulance? Finny craned to look into the bathroom. Where the hell, for that matter, was the blasted attendant?

Five eternal minutes later, Finny shot out of the lounge into the passageway. Jesus, they'd had time to call a dozen rescue units. She went out into the deserted foyer. She could hear the music rising behind the closed doors of the concert hall. What had happened to Bartholomew? Out of the corner of her eyes, she saw Les Trethalwyn exit from the passage entrance on the other side of the hall.

MacKenzie Bartholomew came around the corner. "Miss Aletter." Pallor had made his face roughly the shade of his shirt.

Finny turned on him. "Where've you been? Did you call the paramedics?"

"Miss Aletter, I must talk with you." He grasped her arm and tugged her toward the stairs. "It's most important."

"Are you crazy?" Finny shot a frantic look back over her shoulder toward the women's lounge. "I've got to get back to Twee and—"

"No, you must come with me." He steered her to the stairs.

Finny searched the still-gray face. He was flicking little glances from side to side under heavily frowning brows, and his mouth was tight with strain. Maybe the stress of Twee's illness had stripped his gears. "Did I miss something?" she asked gently. "Don't you think we'd better stay with Twee until the paramedics get here?"

"You're very cool under pressure," Bartholomew said in a flat voice. "I admire that." He started up the empty staircase, pulling her along with him. "You needn't pretend. The paramedics won't be coming."

Finny stumbled over one of the steps, and her mind flashed for an instant to the loose runner on Corinne's stairs. Bartholomew steadied her through the inexorable pull upward. "You don't have to pretend any longer," he repeated. "I assume that Twee told you."

"Told me what? I don't know what you're talking—" Except that, suddenly, she did know. It was what Twee had been saying about looking beyond the surface. And she'd apologized to Herbert for not knowing "he" was involved.

Her mind clicked with admirable, if belated, efficiency. Abigail had mentioned silent partners in the crooked land deal that had destroyed Herbert Garrett. And she, herself, had asked the most pertinent question: how could William Sarandon have pulled off such sleazery while on the bench? It was easy if you had a partner. Me and my shadow . . .

"But why? Why kill Sarandon if you were in it together?" Finny had stopped dead on one of the stairsteps, gawking at him on the step above her.

"He wanted out. He started believing his own press notices—the controversial judge—even started talking about running for the legislature." His voice dripped contempt. "William would have thrown me to the wolves if any hint got out. And of course it would have gotten out." He turned to take another step.

"No." Finny held her ground, pulling back against the tight grasp on her arm. "I don't feel like going with you."

In a smooth, deadly motion, Bartholomew slid his hand into his coat pocket and pulled out a small gun and pointed it at her. She could see little more than the round, dark hole of its barrel. "Yes, you do."

Finny looked wildly around the empty foyer below them. Les had been at the other end of the long room moments before. Where was he now?

Bartholomew's disapproving eyes grew colder. "We are leaving here and you are going to give me the negatives." Finny's arm jerked under his hand and he bared his teeth in what was supposed to be a smile. "Yes, you know all about those pictures, don't you? It was bad enough when that pathetic excuse for a photographer came to me for a payoff. A cheap blackmailer . . ." he trailed off into curses, his hand clamping so tightly on her arm that her fingers tingled.

Finny was remembering all too clearly the details of Mike Guiterrez's injuries. Had Bartholomew inflicted them, or had he hired someone? Did she really want to find out?

"Stop stalling." Bartholomew jerked her arm sharply upward and Finny cried out. "Be quiet."

That night in the kitchen, Finny was thinking starkly. He had been looking for these negatives. "I don't have them," she said.

He stopped, one more step to go, to scan her eyes.

"How could I?" Finny spoke softly, urgently. "I didn't know Guiterrez. What makes you think I have them?"

"Excuse me, senor?"

Bartholomew whirled round. At the top of the stairs was a woman, one of the rest room attendants by the black uniform she wore. She held out an envelope. "Is this what you're looking for?"

Finny bit back a gasp. Bianca Lopez met her gaze for an instant, then looked back at Bartholomew.

He was staring at the envelope. "What are you talking about? What's this—"

"Someone left it for you, senor." She opened up the envelope and took out a photograph, tilting it toward him.

He let go of Finny's arm and snatched at the colored square and the envelope it came from.

Finny had time to take one step up the stairs.

Bianca released the small packet and, in a smooth, deliberate motion, put both hands against MacKenzie Bartholomew's chest and pushed. He cried out as his arms flew upward in fruitless reflex, falling backward, his face frozen in terror.

The muffled swell of music from the concert hall could not drown out the arhythmic thuds his body made as it fell to the bottom of the stairs.

FINISH LINE

FOR YOU, *Jito,* she said silently to her unborn child, and then she turned away. She found a shadowed corner and waited until she could control the shaking of her body.

Now she had to get away.

The sounds from downstairs were getting louder. She pushed herself away from the wall and walked down the middle of the corridor, glancing casually over the rail in time to see Twee Garrett carried out on a stretcher. Several people were gathered around the broken figure at the base of the stairs, and she realized that MacKenzie Bartholomew must be dead. Good.

They would be searching for her soon. She had brought clothes to change into and had left them in the employee lounge. The Aletter woman knew who she was, but with different clothes, if she put her hair up, maybe she could leave unnoticed.

She waited until people began to leave the theater, falling in behind a group going down the stairs. Her eyes flicked over the scene below, catching sight of the Aletter woman, who stood beside a small, old woman in black.

As she watched, a man, the tall police lieutenant, pushed through the revolving door, striding over to the two women, embracing the younger.

Bianca came to the bottom of the stairs and walked toward the door. She glanced to her left and saw Finny Aletter, looking with the tall man at the photographs Miguel had died for. As she passed, Finny looked up, her gaze meeting Bianca's. She nodded, almost imperceptibly.

Bianca walked through the glass doors out into the warm night.

IF IT'S MURDER, CAN DETECTIVE J.P. BEAUMONT BE FAR BEHIND?...

FOLLOW IN HIS FOOTSTEPS WITH FAST-PACED MYSTERIES BY J.A. JANCE

TRIAL BY FURY 75138-0/$3.95 US/$4.95 CAN

IMPROBABLE CAUSE 75412-6/$3.95 US/$4.95 CAN

INJUSTICE FOR ALL 89641-9/$3.95 US/$4.95 CAN

TAKING THE FIFTH 75139-9/$3.95 US/$4.95 CAN

UNTIL PROVEN GUILTY 89638-9/$3.95 US/$4.95 CAN

A MORE PERFECT UNION
75413-4/$3.95 US/$4.95 CAN

DISMISSED WITH PREJUDICE
75547-5/$3.50 US/$4.25 CAN

MINOR IN POSSESSION
75546-7/$3.95 US/$4.95 CAN

Buy these books at your local bookstore or use this coupon for ordering:

Mail to: Avon Books, Dept BP, Box 767, Rte 2, Dresden, TN 38225
Please send me the book(s) I have checked above.
[ ] My check or money order—no cash or CODs please—for $ _____ is enclosed
(please add $1.00 to cover postage and handling for each book ordered to a maximum of three dollars).
[ ] Charge my VISA/MC Acct# _____ Exp Date _____
Phone No _____ I am ordering a minimum of two books (please add postage and handling charge of $2.00 plus 50 cents per title after the first two books to a maximum of six dollars). For faster service, call 1-800-762-0779. Residents of Tennessee, please call 1-800-633-1607. Prices and numbers are subject to change without notice. Please allow six to eight weeks for delivery.

Name _____

Address _____

City _____ State/Zip _____

Jance 4/90